SINGLE ACTION

NELSON NYE

THORNDIKE
CHIVERS

This Large Print edition is published by Thorndike Press, Waterville, Maine USA and by BBC Audiobooks Ltd, Bath, England.
Thorndike Press is an imprint of Thomson Gale, a part of The Thomson Corporation.
Thorndike is a trademark and used herein under license.

LIBRARY OF CONGRESS CATALOGING-IN-PUBLICATION DATA

Nye, Nelson C. (Nelson Coral), 1907–
    Single action / by Nelson Nye.
      p. cm. — (Thorndike Press large print western)
    ISBN-13: 978-0-7862-9134-2 ISBN-10: 0-7862-9134-6 (lg. print : alk. paper)
    1. Large type books. I. Title.
PS3527.Y3355 2006
813'.54—dc22
                                               2006028954

BRITISH LIBRARY CATALOGUING-IN-PUBLICATION DATA AVAILABLE

Published in 2006 in the U.S. by arrangement with Golden West Literary Agency.
Published in 2007 in the U.K. by arrangement with Golden West Literary Agency.

U.K. Hardcover: 978 1 405 63992 7 (Chivers Large Print)
U.K. Softcover: 978 1 405 63993 4 (Camden Large Print)

Printed in the United States of America on permanent paper
10 9 8 7 6 5 4 3 2 1

SINGLE ACTION

CHAPTER 1

Staring in disgust at ink stained fingers, I flung down the broken-nibbed pen, glowering at the heaped-up mound of reports with all the intolerance and bitter frustration any man must feel who'd been buried like me under a smothering avalanche of never-ending papers the whole nine interminable weeks that I'd been squatting here.

A deal of guys, I expect, had me down for lucky to have been taken on after being pulled out of the kind of scrape I had, but I hadn't joined up with Mossman's Rangers to continual ride herd on no dadblasted pen!

I was minded to tell him so.

Arizona these days — if you swallowed what was wrote in them big Eastern dailies — was the last frontier, populated with rustlers, coyotes, high-rolling gamblers, prostitutes and their pimps, horse thieves, back stabbers and seven other kinds of two-legged snakes — and it did, I own, sometimes seem to have more than its rightly just share of such varmints.

What we wanted out here was to get made a state, taken into the Union with some say about things — self-government particular, and the blown-up hogwash peddled by them rags wasn't helping our cause none. Every picayune killing or hanging they got hold of was played up like a major disaster when most of the time folks around here was just as well pleased to be rid of such bastards.

We could be a mite obstreperous — I ain't denying that, and in schoolboard meetings or some matter of assessment pull in forty different directions. But we could pull together, too . . . like fixing roads and blowed-off roofs or tackling a bridge that looked about to wash out. Even the no-accounts throwed in for such frolics, the women pitching in to fetch along the food-stuffs. Like I say, we was all some strong for statehood.

Big thing was the United States Congress — according to the gent we had up there speaking for us — had consented at last to next year give our petition a hearing. Which didn't leave much choice but to put things in order in advance of the delegation we was told they'd be sending to see how ready we was for independence.

Our governor — Murphy — wasn't no-body's fool. He knew we'd got to clean house, really make the dust fly, and that it wasn't no job for local politicos. He called in a man who had no fences to mend, Burt Mossman, the feller that cleaned out the Hashknife outfit. Told him the problems, what had got to be done.

"You've got twelve months to sweep out this scum. You'll organize and head up a statewide police force — same kind of thing they've got over in Texas, and there will be no excuses. Results is all I'm interested in."

Mossman had been authorized to enlist twelve men, these enjoined to furnish both firearms and horseflesh, the Territory pay-ing for what shells they used and, in the field, for their grub. Twelve men, and him-self, to tame and clean up in a fistful of months 113,909 square miles of what them newspaper fellers called "hell with the clacker off."

I guess you'll think Murphy was just about ready for a string of spools. A lot of loud-mouths laughed when they heard about this deal. Cleaning rustlers out of the Blue was one thing. Be easier, they said, for Moss-man's fools to rid the country of Indians and jackrabbits — take a lifetime, they sneered, to round up the owl-hooters infesting the territory.

The odds were against him and in those first weeks bets was being placed in every bar and bordello from Nogales to Kingman, some of the harder-faced characters putting up ten to one. About the only one who didn't have much to say was Burt himself. He never was long on talk.

I picked up my pen and found a new nib for it. Someone, I reckoned, had to do his damn paperwork. You didn't hear nobody laughing now. With four months gone our outfit had made some impressionable inroads, furnishing considerable material for after supper yarning around the cookfires of the cowcamps and anywheres else three-four rannies got together.

A Ranger, they said, could be just about anyone, and strangers all over was being looked at like hawks. I didn't give two whoops how they peered at me if only I could someway get a piece of the action and away from this crippling goddam desk.

I was turning loose of a prodigious sigh when the feel of watching eyes come over me, hauling me round to find Cap's dark face in a weighing look considering me from the door to his office.

"You wantin' me, Captain?" I started to get up.

He waved me back with that skimmed milk stare. "How old are you, Pearly?"

"Eighteen, Cap—" I broke off, flustered. "Well . . . near enough as makes no difference."

He was a hard man to lie to, and stood a while longer shaking his head like a gent facing up to some unwanted truth. "How long you been dogie, son?"

"Ever since that flood on the Aravaipa caught my folks in Tellicum Canyon. You remember that summer when —"

"I remember." He rasped the scrape of a hand across bristles and let go a sigh that was first cousin to mine. "Three years on your own. Reckon that Jaddito business settled you down any?"

I could feel the hot color piling into my cheeks. What he meant was that scrape they had got me out of. There was this girl. A commission dove from one of them saloons that me and this tamale got to pawing sod over. The guy was unarmed but I didn't know that. He reached for something and I let him have it, that .44 slug taking him square between the eyes. Things got right ugly. The Mexkins in that mob was yelling for a rope when one of Cap's boys took me

11

off their hands.

Mossman cleared his throat. It hauled my stare off the floor. "I won't forget that, sir — nor what you done for me."

"Question is did you learn anything."

"I sure hope so, sir."

"That makes two of us," Mossman said dry like, continuing to stand with that doubt in his look. "This outfit's piling up troubles enough without riding herd on one of its own. You've got speed and the eye to make a good man but there's more to police work than gunplay — remember that."

He stared some more with that mouth of his hid behind the mustache sweeping both sides of his jaw. He said, pretty grim, "I dislike sending an untried man into the field. With everyone out I don't have much choice. Even without this trial coming up I . . ." He broke it off, said abruptly, "How well are you known over at Charleston, boy?"

"They don't know me at all," I cried, full of hope. "I've never been nearer to that camp than right here."

He come out of the doorway, propped a hip on my desk. "Bad blood over there, could be a feud building up —"

"But I thought that place was plumb gone to pot. When the Tombstone mines —"

He waved me quiet. "Town's come back. From the little I've been told it's a tougher boot now than Tombstone was in its palmiest days." He considered me some more. Blew the breath from his cheeks. "I need a gun over there *but I don't want one that's going off half cocked!*"

"You can count on me! I won't let you down, sir!"

I meant it, too, but he heard the excitement bubbling through my words. Not that he'd have missed it if I'd never opened my mouth. Those steel sharp eyes could catch anything.

But all he said was, "Get your stuff together, boy," and turned away with a shake of the head. "When you're ready to ride," he threw back at the door, "stop by and I'll brief you."

CHAPTER 2

Charleston, as the crow files, was no tolerable great distance from Mossman's headquarters at Bisbee where he had a meat packing plant with a feller named Cudahy. By road it was farther. On the back of a horse you'd spend the bulk of one day without you changed off or run his hoofs plumb into the ground.

Way I went, traveling on orders to come in from the east, there wasn't no roads till a man got to Gleeson, an up and down a stretch of twenty odd miles beyond the east end of the "town too tough to die."

The first night I spent bedded down in my clothes underneath two blankets right out in the brush, sung to sleep by coyotes with a bitter wind whooping off the Swisshelm Mountains. You wouldn't think in mid summer it could get so damn cold. The second night was no warmer, but I had the lights of Tombstone to look at and, while these did not noticeably increase my comfort, at least they inspired in me a tingly appreciation of my own importance for knowing on the morrow I'd be at my destination ready to prove my fitness for the trust Cap had placed in me.

He hadn't give me no definite orders, not sure himself what this was all about. Nobody'd sent out a squawk for help. What little he'd picked up had been roundabout — mostly third or fourth hand, a word or two here, another one there, some unfathomable looks — nothing a man could put a finger flat on.

"Could be making a molehill out of a ant's house. One thing I do know," Cap said to me. "Two-Pole Pumpkin has been buying up a slew of two-bit outfits, none of 'em touching. If I found myself between two of those spreads I would sure as hell be doing some tall thinking. One thing it's done is push up values. It's also fetched in a raft of new people. Town's population has tripled in six months, which is enough in itself to merit our attention."

"Some kind of squeeze play?"

"That's for you to find out. There's bad blood over there," Cap said grimly. "Whatever's on the boil I figure it wouldn't take much to kick the lid off and spew up into some pretty ugly doin's."

Charleston was nine miles southwest of Tombstone, ideally located for purposes of crime. It was on the San Pedro, which made it powerful handy for road agents and others hankering to hide their tracks. Once in the stream, all traces could be obliterated by the fugitive turning up or down and not coming out till he found some ledge — of which there was plenty — that would hide his prints. There was likewise numerous creeks and washes, with the banks of the river high enough that any horsebacker using it wouldn't be seen till after he'd got a good piece off.

That whole country had been pocked by gophering prospectors and overgrazed besides. Gophering was a kind of mining where some guy on a shoestring would put down a shoveled hole on spec and, when nothing come of it, pack up and leave. It would take a large chunk of that kind of graze to support a spread that had to make it on cattle. It just didn't make sense they'd checkerboard a range without some kind of skulduggery in the offing. I could see well enough why Mossman figured he'd better have someone keeping an eye out.

The Two-Pole Pumpkin Land & Cattle Company was a British owned outfit headquartering in Wyoming. They could be hunting winter range, pushed by the snows and cold weather of that country, or they could be taking up land because it was cheap. It was plain Cap Mossman took a grimmer view. Already, he said, they'd sent down a crew and resident manager to vent and rebrand the cows they'd acquired with these picked-up parcels. Feller's name was Lockhart. He had opened an office in town, Cap said, though what for no one had told him.

My best approach, seemed like to me, was to hit this Lockhart up for a job. Cap wasn't too sure. "Look around a bit first. Get your ear to the ground. You won't be gettin' much help from that bunch — or me."

I didn't need to be reminded. He had all he could handle right there in Bisbee, not to mention the paperwork. A Ranger was a man with guts and a horse. He had a heap in common with them Knights of the Round Table and, though scenery and times was considerable different, more or less the same job, the righting of wrongs. He was the scourge of evil doers, the strong right hand of Justice.

The twenty-first legislature, harried by Murphy, had authorized his calling, given him legal status and established his pay at one hundred dollars per month, a handsome stipend in 1901. Two bits would get you a pretty fair meal, and death by violence was so commonplace no one thought twice about the risks that went with it. You could get killed just as quick keeping shop if you got careless.

I went through Tombstone at five the next morning with the sun just climbing above the hills.

Didn't look much like the hell-roaring camp it was said to have been during the reign of the Earps. I passed a string of ore wagons setting out there in Allen Street, left right where the mules had been uncoupled, and looking not much more abandoned than the paintless buildings cheek by jowl at either side. The Oriental's gutted innards strewed with rubbish and busted-up furniture showed thick with dust through the shards of broken windows.

The Crystal Palace, in front of which Virgil Earp had gone down, was apparently intact and still doing business though I saw no one in it as I rode past. Flapping blinds and doors hung askew from more than half the shops. Warner Brothers' store was boarded up and padlocked. Vogan's Bowling Alleys looked presentable enough, though likewise empty at this early hour.

The Alhambra was dead and, two doors down, the Occidental Saloon looked like a mare's nest, and the Cosmopolitian Hotel, alongside, looked as blank of face as its one-time rival cattycornered across the bordering Fourth. Made you feel, by grab, like you was staring at the corpses of unburied dead. Closing them mines had sure played hell.

I jogged along past the Can Can Building with its boarded-up Can Can Restaurant and on out of town without once stopping. Remembering things that was past, I just hadn't the heart to get out of my saddle. History had been made on that street and its present appearance was a hard thing to see. I was anxious to get the taste of it out of my system and more anxious still to get where I was going. I figured to make Cap proud of me and I sure didn't want to miss out on no fireworks. I knew without giving full sense to it then that being fast with a gun was not the first thing Cap looked for in a Ranger. And he was right. I know that now. Half an hour later I was looking at Charleston. Riding past the abandoned smelter and dropping down through the arroyo I was — despite what Cap had told me — considerable astonished to see so much activity in a town that had depended on the Tombstone mines. Seemed like people was

19

on the move everywhere, afoot, on horseback and in half a dozen kinds of wheeled rigs. New buildings were going up in five or six places, the main street a scene of bustling activity.

With a knee hooked round the horn I sat there spinning me up a smoke while I looked this thriving community over and wondered at the optimism fetched in by outside capital. I counted three wagonloads of lumber on the go and just below Gird's mill I glimpsed the canvas tops of more than thirty tents. Cap had called the turn. This place was booming, no doubt about it.

In its heyday Charleston had led a rather checkered career. Burt Alvord, the prank-loving train robber, had once been a constable or deputy here, along with a lot of other desperate characters. As Mossman had pointed out, it had an ideal climate for the blossoming of crime. West and north was a region that in the old days had been infested with Apaches. Straight north in the Cherrycow Mountains, Cochise had had his stronghold. South, and not too many miles away, was the Mexican border. It seemed still a good place to make a getaway from.

I considered the San Pedro, eighty feet from bank to bank, shallow now but with a good run of water. In Alvord's time it had been frequently said that if one came into this place looking for trouble he wouldn't have to hunt very long to get a bellyful. I peered back at Gird's mill. Here the crude ore from the Tombstone mines had been converted into shiny bars of rich metal — a natural mecca for stick-up artists and others of the get-rich-quick persuasion. There was Gird's office with its roof fallen in, built of adobe, its walls three feet thick.

Freighting ore from Tombstone to Charleston had been something of a problem; a lot of things had been tried and found too expensive. Finally some jasper named Durkee had took over the contracts, and after that there was profit. He'd thrown a party one night to celebrate the deal and from what I've been told it must have been a stem-winder. Women and gambling — wine, brandy, rum. When these had run out those still on their feet had taken to putting down soldier whisky; two swigs of that were claimed to knock a man sideways at sixty yards without a miss. This had been a blue shirt brawl, the while collared crowd had been stopped at the door. The freighters, mostly Texicans, had broke up the shindig in a free-for-all that a man could date time by.

Frank Stillwell had once kept a livery

stable here. Charleston was the Red Dog of Alfred Henry Lewis' Wolfville tales. James Wolf, who had done a little of everything and hung on here a deal longer than most, was said to have loaned Lewis his collection of newspaper clippings used as background for Lewis' stories.

When Gird's smelter was painting the night skies red, the town had boasted four stores, two hotels, several blacksmith shops and a flock of saloons and honkytonks where the cheapest thing was said to have been the lives of patrons. About three hundred people had been living here then and, from what I could see, there was at least that many busy trotting around now.

In the old days, jail had been a hole in the ground, an abandoned prospect partly filled and with a big stake embedded in the very middle of it to which prisoners had been chained till they could be taken to Tombstone. Not a few of those buggers had had ugly things thrown at them.

There had, originally, been about twenty-five adobe buildings. The place had nearer fifty now, counting the new outlying ones put up with lumber. Scott's store had been reopened.

There was a story going the rounds in Bisbee, that Jim Wolf, asked what he had done with his land, said, "Lord, I sold off all of it, but conserved ten acres for my own use. I'm fixin' to build a congregated iron house there and live on it." His questioner said, "Don't you mean *corrugated?*" "No," Jim says, "I mean just what I said, I got as much right to make new words as Nora Webster."

There had used to be a flagpole in the center of town which had been the scene of several prominent fracases, but I didn't see any sign of it now. There was a new general store in competition with Scott's and, apparently, getting most of the trade, if a man was to judge by the horses and rigs.

One old-timer sure to be around was Jim Burnett who'd been J.P. at Charleston since time out of mind. Wolf said of him that he always carried and could use a sixshooter with speed and precision, hence, "there was a vast amount of law and some semblance of order in his particular vicinity at all times."

Jim Wolf, as you've maybe surmised, had considerable to say on practically everything. He hung out these days at Bisbee and was a perambulating authority on whichever subject was tackled. One story he told about Burnett and Charleston concerned a certain loudmouthed saloonkeeper who was disturbing the community's siesta. Judge Burnett and a constable went around to the place, opened court and levied a fine of fifty dollars. On being paid, Judge B. got into a poker game and lost the fifty *muy pronto.* Bogy Red — the constable of those days — being plenty smart, began a fresh argument with the proprietor which, soon as the latter raised his voice, Judge B. rose up and assessed him another fifty. This didn't go much further than the first, but when Bogy Red headed again for the saloonkeeper, the same, which was no fool, began industriously blowing out the lights, but with never a peep of complaint coming out of him.

With the closing of the mines and the end of its chief revenue, Charleston had begun to come apart at the seams. The Mexkins took over, living in tents and abandoned stores and the roundabout shacks of former mill workers. A good share of the place had been wrecked for firewood, according to Mossman. Puffing my smoke I looked to spot which of the buildings I could see appeared old enough to have survived their rowdy past. Toting these up didn't need any more than the fingers of one hand, and, except for Scott's — still in use — and the relics of Gird's mill yonder, what was left wouldn't have give decent shelter to a one-eyed gopher.

Sam Katzenstein's was gone. And Horrera & McClure that, with Springer & Hacke, had once carried stocks valued at close to a hundred thousand. Nothing much appeared to have hung on but a packrat population of Mexkins and possibly a handful of die-hard ranchers still scraping a living from the Huachuca Mountains — Cap had said I'd likely see a few of them.

I rode on in, presently stopping in front of Scott's. The porch roof looked about ready to fall in, and there was nobody holding down the benches by the door. A wrinkled old Apache had one blanketed shoulder propping up a post and, when I got down, he roused himself enough to grunt something about 'tobbac' and stick out a hand.

I give him my Durham and went on in.

The place was dark enough inside to've been the cave of Ali Barber. Strings of chili peppers hung from the rafters along with some moldering harness and headstalls, probably left over from the original stock. A bell tinkled someplace and a skinny Mex girl came in from the back to find out what I wanted. Except for dust, the sagging shelves was pretty near bare. I spied some moth eaten blankets and perhaps three dozen cans of bully beef with faded fly-specked labels. "Bull Durham," I said, and she fetched me a sack from under the counter. "Trade pretty brisk?"

She picked up my coin with a twist of the lips. *"No bueno por nada."*

With her scrubbed clean face and pulled-back hair, you'd of swore she hadn't seen above a dozen summers. Then she tipped back her head with a flash of white teeth. "You cowboy?" The look she give me was older than Adam.

A stage rattled past throwing dust through the door.

It darkened again with a chink of spurs as I half swung to follow the lifting stab of her widening gaze.

Against that outside glare about all I could see was his broad black shape under a Texas hat with the ears standing out from his head like handles.

A plumb fool would of felt the menace that come in with him. It lifted the hairs along the back of my neck as a hand sloshed up to stop against his hip. "Where the hell's your ol' man?"

Coming fully round I went back a step to get him away from that doorhole light and saw the grimy hide vest and black wool shirt, the tobacco bulged jaw — the whole bullypuss look of him.

I said: "Who wants to know?" and felt the

hard thrust of his insolent stare.

"Stay out of this, sport."

His arrogance was a cramp in my gut, his contempt as intolerable as the way he ignored me to put a hard grin on the girl. He clanked up to the counter dragging rowels to stand, fists on hips, like he owned the damn joint and everything in it — particularly her. "Where is he?"

She was shrunk against the shelving, eyes like two burnt holes in the bedsheet pallor of her frozen cheeks. "He ees not here —"

Not taking her word for it, rounding the counter he ripped down a blanket, flinging it aside, to rampage through the back of the place, returning with an irritable scowl.

"We'll find him, by Gawd —"

"But, señor, 'ees 'as done nothing!"

"That's his worry. He was told t' clear out."

"Does these Two-Pole Pumpkin 'ave to 'ave *everytheeng*?"

"Don't have to, but goin' to." His insolence rummaged her from head to toe, working back up her length with a brightening attention. Suddenly grinning, he reached for her. "Be nice to me, kid, an' —"

"Leave her alone!"

The shape of him stiffened. His head swirled around to give me an ogling from across one hunched shoulder. "Get lost," he growled, and reached again for the girl.

She came out of her fright with a scream, tried to run. The big bugger chuckled. He snaked out an arm, caught the back of her dress at the neck and yanked, tearing the thing pretty near clean off her.

CHAPTER 3

I never stopped to do no thinking.

Hate rushed through me so fierce and every resolve I had come with was dashed from my head. Through a red fog I went for him, left hand scrabbling to grab his right shoulder. He shook me off, paying no more notice than I'd of give a damn nit.

I grabbed again, spun him round on braced legs and caught him with a wallop fetched up from my bootstraps.

He went crosseyed into them shelves with a crash. His hat come off. One of them cans filled with beef off the top banged into his noggin and he slid out of sight like a calf in a boghole.

I blew out my cheeks feeling righteous as Moses.

While I was rubbing my knuckles, wondering if I'd broke something, I hear this gasp like a sob from the girl. She's over there leaning, filled with horror, peering back of

29

the counter.

"He ain't dead," I said, "if that's what's itchin' you."

She give me a terrible look, eyes juning round like she'd been stuffed with splinters, every one of 'em afire. She started sputtering Spanish, the words tumbling over each other like frijoles popping from a burst-bottomed sack. Maybe she seen how bewildered I was. She broke off, eyes widening, to clutch what was left of that dress to the front of her.

"But . . . to *strike* heem!" she cried. "The chief man of Señor Lock'art!" You'd of thought the whole damn sky was coming down. She filled her lungs up again. "They weel *keel* my papa!"

I couldn't see the connection. Her papa hadn't hit him.

But somewhere in her jabber I recollected them ranches Two-Pole Pumpkin had been picking up for peanuts. I begun to get the drift.

Seemed like her father had been told to pack and git. The old man hadn't give it a quick enough attention. Bullheadedness, it looked like, run in her family. "So what's the beef?" I cut in to ask. "Thought you told Handsome Harry" — I jerked a thumb toward the counter — "he hadn't done nothin'."

She said he hadn't. But too many Mexkins was buying their grub and gewgaws here. The Big Man, apparently, couldn't abide competition.

It sounded pretty crazy. Even to me.

This girl was quick. "You don't believe?"

Eyes big as slop pails she was practically standing on my arches. "Ees no bueno, these man." She glommed onto my arm, so tight I could feel the shakes going through her. "Keel — all the time keel, keel, keel!"

"Now wait a minute," I said, growling it kind of account of the flush I'd worked up from her nearness. "That don't wash. If they been gunnin' guys down right an' left the way you tell it —"

"Hoh!" She looked her contempt. "You theenk pair'aps I make these op!" She grabbed away her hand and herself along with it. Her eyes said I was a plain plumb fool; and I guessed I was, taking a poke at that guy, laying myself wide open. I had a vision of Cap which didn't help none, either.

She got the hair off her cheek with a toss of the head, indignation quivering each breath. She must of caught my glance straying off towards the counter and, just that quick, all the fright was back in her. With a

31

jumpety gasp she took off past the blanket that lay crumpled on the floor from Two-Pole Pumpkin's impatience.

I stepped over to have another look.

He was still out cold but you could see his muscles was beginning to twitch, and he wasn't no kind to stamp your boot and yell 'boo' at. He had a horsebacker's legs but from the waist on up was built like that Big-feller's blacksmith my Ma used to tell about. I could guess what was like to be most on his mind if he come to with me cluttering the view.

I heard the slam of a door. So the girl had lit out, which was probably the smartest thing for me to do too. Still studying on it I considered him some more and, just to be on the safe side, reached down and lifted the gun from his shell belt. What, after all, could I say to the bastard? I couldn't well tell him I was here on Cap's orders.

A Ranger never advertised his calling. I'd had that drummed into me long enough to know. Another thing he didn't was get mixed up in things that was none of his nevermind. Girls! By God, Cap would bust my surcingle!

I didn't know what to do hardly. It wasn't that I was reaching for any rusty old halo, but with that blood on his face and the thoughts he was going to wake with I couldn't see that I would gain a heap postponing the inevitable.

He was groaning now.

I set my butt on the counter and waited for him to find me.

It didn't take long! He come off the floor like a half skun cat. One paw slapped his holster, pure murder glinting from the cracks of his stare when he spotted his shooter peering at him from my lap.

"Take it easy," I said. "You maybe been the victim of a slight misunderstandin'. After all, these things do happen."

I didn't have to be told they didn't happen to him — his eyes done that with compound interest. I thought right then he was going to jump me anyhow. Maybe I looked meaner than I felt. He took a hitch in his temper but a hair could of held it better.

"What are you, fella — some kinda nut?"

Any fool could of seen he wasn't forgetting it.

"Put yourself in my place," I told him. "Sure looked like you was askin' for it."

I could see he wasn't going to buy that. I said doggedly, trying to make it reasonable, "What I done was only natural —"

"Why you goddam scissorsbill! You know

who I am!"

"I do now," I said. "That's why I waited. Thought you should know I made a mistake."

It didn't seem to rid him of much of his wild look, so I told him, "No hard feelin's on my part," and tossed him his gun.

He wasn't no fumbler — I'll say that for him. Nor did he waste any time laying down his character. He picked that rod out of the air slick as bear grease, took snap aim and straightaway started triggering.

Nothing happened, of course. I had its teeth in my pocket.

"Luck sure ain't ridin' your shirt tail this mornin'," I waggled my head at him. "You disappoint me, mister. A clout in the kisser ought to've learnt you some manners —"

I hauled in my head. The flung gun whacked against the wall, hit the floor with a clatter in a dribble of mud plaster. Still eyeing him I sighed. "You've done curdled my hope in the future of humanity."

Practically frothing at the mouth he looked about to climb my frame barehanded. Whipping the hogleg from my holster I told him: "Come ahead."

He was wild all right, but not completely foolish. He stopped, cateyed and careful, oozed back into his boots. "You've made the head of the class," I nodded. "Take off whenever you're a mind to."

He stood a couple moments longer, committing my look to some special place reserved and sacred to the memory of disasters.

It was dollars to doughnuts I'd hear more of this anon.

CHAPTER 4

Sure I'd been a mite impulsive, carried away you might say by things that wasn't, strictly speaking, my concern — yet I couldn't, looking back, pin too much blame on myself. What gent with a ounce of red blood in his gizzard was going to stand by while that fiesty walloper . . .

"Hell!" I said, and hauled my hip off the counter.

Just the same I had put my foot in it. From here on out I'd be a marked man in his book. Any chance I'd had to get on with that outfit was dead right now as last year's grass.

There was a number of things I might reasonably do, but sticking round town wasn't one of them. I picked up the can that had fell on his head, left a coin on the counter and went out to my horse.

No one had bothered him. The Injun was gone. I put the beef in my slicker and climbed into the saddle. If bad blood was fixing to boil in these parts it only made sense somebody in this basin was not of a mind to kiss the ass of British arrogance. Which, by my count, made two of us.

I didn't even have to locate this outfit, just circulate is all — so maybe I hadn't got off so wrong at that. From what I had seen of Lockhart's segundo he was not the kind to hide his hate under a bushel. Soon's the word got around I could expect a proposition.

Having reached this conclusion I took to the river. Nothing wrong I could see with lifting a page from the owlhooter's manual. That feller had looked the kind to stomp his own snakes, but one thing I'd learnt wrastlen Cap's reports: All else being equal the gunsmoke breed, where they had any choice, generally cottoned to odds that was in their favor. I didn't reckon I was fixed to take on half the town.

I turned upstream in the direction of Fairbank and Curtis, Cap's cautions right then looming large in my mind — not, of course, that I was scairt of that bastard. But I could see it might be best to stick with rules as much as possible.

I stayed in the river for the most of three miles. There was water in it — plenty.

Sometimes it come over my gelding's hocks; twice it reached his belly, even looked like we might have to swim. Then I found this ledge and we clambered out. A kind of trail, not too recently traveled, followed the east bank through the greasewood and occasional thickets of thorny mesquite all decked out now with their clusters of beans that a man could live on if you come right down to it.

The sun was hot. We worked up a sweat without half trying. In its smoldering glare I could trace the dark line of the Dragoon Mountains off north and east where they shimmered in the film like a gob of grape jelly. Off to the left Apache Peak stuck up with Granite Peak in its shadow showing blue through the haze.

Once away from the river this was pretty dry country, dun, green-flecked where wind had packed the sand against brush in a clutter of humpbacked islands. But now everything lay quiet as the bottom of a shaft.

This was not good range in its present shape. The signs of overgrazing was everywhere apparent. There was feed, but not the kind to carry more than one cow in twenty acres.

One thing I didn't need to keep an eye peeled for was Injuns. With Geronimo out of the country most of his kinfolk was on the reservation getting fat on government subsidy. But it was still good country to stay awake in. Considering the bustle going on in Charleston there'd be plenty of hardcases riding the hills in search of opportunity — which could be one of the things that had Cap worried.

If real trouble broke out there'd be plenty to whoop things up, working their guns for the highest bidder, about as reliable as a mailorder watch. A feller owning cattle in such a situation could damn well be ruint in mighty short order. The havenots always got the best of such hassles.

The sun was heeling into mid-afternoon when I spotted a scrabble of buildings ahead and pulled up in some brush to give the place the once over.

I was sure this wasn't Fairbank. It had more the look of a hog ranch, and likewise wasn't big enough. Besides the Southern Pacific went through Fairbank on its way to Douglas, and there was no sign of rails or water tower. It had to be some kind of deadfall, I reckoned, some crosstrails bar dependent on the trade of squatters and drifters. A powerful good place to get a knife up your gullet.

I shrugged the thought away. *Keep your*

ear to the ground, Cap had said; and there was no better chance, it seemed to me, to pick up any talk that was going the rounds than a place where men paused to rest a weary elbow.

True, there wasn't much likelihood of anything important being aired before a stranger. Trust, I imagined, would be in short supply, but my horse could use the rest and my throat would feel some better for having the dust cut out of it.

I rode on in. The nearer I got the more it looked like a road ranch or station of the sort put up to accommodate stage travel. As a matter of fact it was a tumbledown ruin. The dilapidated buildings, warped and paintless, half askew, were in worse shape than abandoned Fort Bowie. The only kept-up thing in sight as I swung down was the pole corral just off the main structure. Strong enough by the look to pen a herd of wild mustangs. A couple of rugged built geldings, half asleep in the sun, stood inside swishing flies, the only living things in sight.

A weatherbeaten sign, plainly homemade and pretty well chewed up by time, carried the one word Saloon with S put on backwards. The porch roof sagged, the plank steps, protesting my weight, groaned as

40

lugubrious as a banshee with green apple colic.

I yanked open the floppy, much-patched screen and stepped into the trapped heat of a long low room whose most distinguishing feature — not counting the dispensary — was a unlit iron-tired wagonwheel chandelier. The place smelled of stale booze and departed tobacco smoke.

A garish fly-spotted print in full color of an undressed, plump and frolicsome cutie hung over the bar in lieu of a mirror. The broad shelf underneath it, well coated with dust, held a lidless cigar box and three mummified stogies.

Curling my lip I called. "Anybody home?"

Nothing returned but a roomful of silence. If that shelf had been stocked I'd of helped myself. As it was I just waited. When my patience give out I fisted my gun and played hob on the bar top.

I'd about reached the point of looking behind it when a big scowling bruiser come in from the back, wiping his hands on a soggy rag. "Chrissake, Jack, you hev t' wake up the baby?"

I opened my mouth and then, quite gently, closed it. No point taking it out on him. "Sorry," I grunted, still grappling my urges.

41

"Reckon that sign is some older than horse turds."

"If you come here t' gab —"

"I'll settle for a drink."

He shoved a fist under the bar and come up with a bottle, planking the thumb-marked glass down beside it. Still scowling, he said: "That'll be four bits."

I whistled and gulped.

"You think this stuff grows on bushes?"

I put out the money and poured me a slug. It must have been crossed with a streak of stray lightning. While I was trying to get back my breath there was horse sounds outside, then a mumble of voices. Somebody laughed.

The barkeep and me swapped crusty glances. A rock face hauled from the nearest mountain could have been quicker read than anything found in that sullen look. I swept glass and bottle far enough down the bar to keep him in sight while I waited for whatever lurked beyond that wabbly screen.

Two rannies in dust powdered range duds shoved through, splitting to stop braced at either side of the door while they took me in from hocks to briskit. Quick, quiet and thorough. The apron, visibly relaxing, caught up his rag and got to work on the bar while the shorter of the pair, unhingeing the hat from his unsheared mop of taffy colored hair, began whacking the dust from the front of his outfit. The paunchy one, snorting, moved up to the bar. "Well, how's tricks? They been keepin' you humpin'?"

I couldn't be sure how the thing had been managed but it struck me as plain this pair had been signaled, which was food in itself for considerable thought.

"No tricks, no humpin'," the barkeep growled. "Business has gone to hell in a handcart — wife wants t' pull out."

And the short guy said, "What's a feller have to do t' git a drink in this place?"

The barkeep threw a bitter look in my direction. "If you're through with that bottle, Jack, send it back."

I filled the glass again and give the bottle a shove, pleased to see it stop square in front of them. The paunchy guy hefted it, took a long belt and handed it to the skinny buck.

"Any work in these parts for a trail weary pilgrim?"

Barkeep and the pot-gut paid no more attention than I'd of give a shoe lace drummer. But the skinny buck, turning, regarded me solemn. "What kinda work, stranger?"

Something about him caught hold of my notice and a whisper of caution began to work through me. But a feller gets nowhere if he don't talk up. I said, "A job is a job when a guy's down to hunger," and left him to figure it any way he would.

He looked at the bottle. "Drifters right now is a dollar a dozen." He took a pull from the nozzle, watching me while he sloshed it around, finally swallowing. He grinned. "If you're a specialist, mister . . ." and let it hang there, watching.

"I know which end of the cows gets the grass."

The other two pulled their heads apart. The belly stared at me and told his pardner, "Let's mosey."

Long Hair reluctant like set down the bottle. "Whyn't you try Fletch Dowlin?" he called over his shoulder while the other guy prodded him towards the door.

After they'd got off the steps I asked the barkeep, "Who's Fletch Dowling?" but he wasn't having any. "You got the price of that second slug?"

I fished out two quarters and shoved them over. He held up the bottle. "You want any more of this?"

I showed him the glass in my hand, two-thirds full. "What I want —" I said, but he wasn't listening.

"If it's all right with you I'll git back to the Missus —"

44

"By grab," I snarled, giving him a look down the tube of my shooter, "you'll leave at your peril. There's worse things in this life than a jawin' woman, an' one of 'em," I said, tapping the bar edge, "is lookin' right at you!"

From a face shades greener than a moldy cheese his eyes stuck out like knobs on a stick.

"Now," I said, making sure he was listening, "who's this Dowlin' an' where-at do I find him?"

CHAPTER 5

No question about him being scairt. His eyes rolled like a stallion bronc's and by the sweat on his cheeks he looked about to heave everything but the kitchen sink. Whatever it was, something else had him worried a heap worse than my gun.

Nothing I tried would open his jaws and at last in disgust I climbed onto my horse.

There seemed bound to have been more to this than I'd cottoned. That pair had showed up to look me over and they must have been fetched on some beforehand rigged signal, but this was far as I could see into it.

I hadn't even learned who them two fellers was, though I could make a good guess about that bardog's main business. What he had here was some sort of hideyhole for guys on the dodge, a layover maybe for movers and cow stealers. That corral was too big, too stout for the rest of it. Didn't seem like to me he could be working for Lockhart. This place seemed too far off the traveled roads.

But just to satisfy myself, soon as I reckoned I'd got completely out of sight, I quit the riverbank to bend a wide loop through the roundabout hills. Leastways that was what I set out to do.

And didn't turn up any sign of that pair. What I did come onto — and considerable quicker than it had been in mind — was the tracks of driven cattle, bound like an arrow for the place I'd just shook the dust of. I followed them far enough to fetch into sight the roofs of them buildings.

Kind of surprised me they'd be so open about it, the cow stealing breed being generally more furtive. It was possible, of course, these weren't stolen cattle — but the odds looked mighty thin.

It come to me there was a way to find out. Wheeling my horse, still keeping an eye peeled, I set out to track down the source of these critters. Not that I set too much store by my chances.

The sun by now was considerable lower, scarce over two foot above the south slopes of Granite Peak, a mass of purplish shadows maybe forty miles west.

I was still riding sign when it dropped out

47

of sight. I didn't know how far I'd come from the river but a half hour later — and I'd been more or less figuring on something like this — I come onto a batch of black lava rocks where there wasn't enough sign left to trip up an ant. This malpais stretched far as I could peer, ridge on tumbled ridge of it, desolate and barren as the bed of some dead sea. Take a army of scouts to unravel a trail through that kind of going.

One thing I had learned in my weeks with Cap Mossman: a Ranger never yelled calf rope. The fellers Cap picked didn't have no quit in 'em.

I wasn't about to camp in this place. I took a long look around and struck out straight across it — seemed as good a way as any. Took me an hour to get clear of them rocks. The far side was something different. Didn't look no better for ranching than the overgrazed scrub around that crosstrails saloon, but the hills swung in closer. They was higher, barer, more rugged. I didn't see no sign of them cow tracks, but there was a trail of sorts making towards a notch where the nearest two hills come down into the desert, and that I struck out for.

The light was getting pretty poor for shooting when I come out of the pass, but not so dark I couldn't see what was before me. A five strand fence. And no gate in sight.

It was what lay beyond that caught my eye. A broad basin or pocket pretty well rimmed by hills, lush and green as a cowman's dreams; windmill towers scattered round all over and, maybe three miles off, the headquarter buildings of whatever outfit was ranching it.

I peered again at the fence, hog tight and horse high. A sign square in front of me, nailed by two posts big round as my legs, said:

WALKING M RANCH
No Trespassing

Didn't seem like a man had ought to cut that kind of fence — not me anyway. That was supposed to be concerned with *stopping* trouble, not starting it.

The flank of the pass, straight up as a cliff, closed off any chance of heading off to the right; to the left however, the hill fell away to leave a passage maybe twenty yards wide. So I went that way, not thinking exactly, not free and easy either. Disturbed enough that I rode with cocked six-shooter fisted in my lap, both eyes slatted at the deepening shadows. Ten years ago — hell's fire, less than that! — this had been the stomping ground of Apaches, but it was something worse than them that had its claws in me now.

Don't ask me what. I hadn't the foggiest.

I lectured myself this was downright silly, foolish as a kid afraid to sleep with the light out. Calling myself seven kinds of a nitwit didn't help a damn bit. The farther I went the more spooky I got. Each dropping hoof-plop seemed to whisper, *Go back!*

I'd been scairt before but nothing like this.

Danger rode that fenceline with me, deadly as the cat-soft padding of a stalking puma. It was a wildness in the curdled gloom. That goddam fence seemed to go on forever.

A night wind moved up out of this basin, strong with the smells of damp earth and pink-barked trees. Every blob of bush or boulder appeared in my confusion to be the lurking shape of some crouched-over gun fighter just waiting to catch me square in his sights.

Only, of course, nothing happened. There was no such critter.

I come at last to a gate. It was chained and padlocked! How long I sat my saddle in a blister of resentment I got no idea. A pile of things went through my head, including the rights of private property, but I was damned if I would follow that fence another lick.

Pulling over close enough to see what I was aiming at, I held out my .44 and put a slug against that jumbo sized padlock where I figured it would do the most good.

It done a bangup job.

The lock fell off in three, four pieces. The racket of that shot slammed around through the hills like hell wouldn't have it while I sat, stiff as froze grease, thinking how Cap would be like to take such doings and expecting any moment to catch the sound of hurried hoofpounds.

Nothing changed. No alarm went up.

My fist closed tighter around the gun. It was full dark now and quiet as a tomb with the last whimpering echo fallen into stillest silence. I tried to think where I had seen them buildings. I couldn't locate even the faintest gleam of light.

I leaned over, pulled loose the heavy links of the chain, edged the gelding through and, still bent, pushed the heavy gate shut, anchoring it there with four clanking turns. I had already pushed my gun back in leather. I got it out again, poked out the spent shell and thumbed in a fresh load. No telling what I was like to run into, but with a mind full of bristles I aimed to be ready.

I kneed the gelding into a walk. Figuring his smeller to be better than mine, I let him pick his own course now, confident of his ability to find the nearest habitation. That's one thing about a horse. They can nose out water if there's any water around.

I didn't worry overmuch about that busted lock. What I did keep close watch for was a bunch of armed and angry men, an irascible owner or trouble hunting segundo, any one of which could be inclined to shoot first and talk later. I remembered that sign; I'd be reckoned fair game.

My horse whickered soft like. Peering ahead, I saw buildings, squat black boxes shoving out of the swirl of shadows. I hadn't seen earlier but the one group of such, so this had to be it.

Pulled up I done more looking, a considerable pile of it without getting nowhere. The heel of my hand fell against my shooter and, careful as a boiled owl negotiating stairs, my fingers caught hold and tipped up the barrel.

Not reassured but at least more ready for whatever this night or this place meant to sling at me, I edged my claybank nearer, gloom closing round me like the drawstrings of a sack.

We passed a hoofshaper's leanto, the back

end of a barn — I could tell what it was by the smells draped around it. Any damn fool would know a bunkhouse when he saw it.

I stopped again.

All this while I'd kept a hand on the gelding's muzzle, expecting with every breath I drew to have some other nag belt up a greeting. A quiet thick as this was nothing a guy would pick from choice.

I thought maybe I oughtn't to have come here. At least I could of waited till daylight; but I was stuck with it now. We wasn't ten foot from the side of that bunk shack and it just wasn't natural not to hear grunts and snores.

Not even a goddam cricket chirped.

That shot. Were they all out hunting? Had it pulled the whole crew? With that much commotion you'd think the house would be lit up.

Maybe I had ought to look around for some horses. But the surest way, plainly, was to call out, announce myself.

I paused to think about that, but in the end I done it.

"Anybody home?"

It come out louder than I'd aimed for. Like a rock dropped into a deep water pool. But nothing come back.

Too jumpy to set still I kneed the claybank toward the house and could tell by the way his ears was cocked, he didn't like this either.

I stopped him by the porch and got down and stood there peering at the windows flanking that shut front door, both hands in plain sight and both of them empty.

Looked like neck meat or nothing.

I stepped onto the porch and not stopping to swallow, put four knuckles hard against the door.

It should of woke the dead but nobody answered. I tried the latch, pushed, and the door swung open.

"Hello — hello!" I called again, and, totting up the risk, fetched a match from my hat, run it down my pantsleg and raised it quick.

CHAPTER 6

I half looked for the dark to be filled with crouching hombres but all I could see was this big empty room.

Sure, there was furnishings, boughten stuff mostly — table and chairs with horsehair backs and a horsehair sofa and off in one corner a pale rolltop desk. I reached out the match to the nearest lamp and, old habits strong, broke what was left and shoved it into a pocket.

Chimney settled, I turned up the wick, held it arm high for a quick squint around. I went through the layout, the whole five rooms of it, and they was all like the front, furnished bachelor style and, just as obviously, empty — I even poked through the closets.

I'm frank to say it had me fighting my hat. Where was the owner and the rest of his outfit, the crew it took to run this spread? The cook ought to be here. I set the lamp on the table, still lit, and went out through the back. Took getting used to, the black of that dark with its jasmine of horses and half glimpsed corrals phantom stretched beyond a stovepiped shack that was almost certainly cook's domain.

But there was nobody in it. I went to the trouble of making sure and then, like the rest, found the corrals empty too. I moved round to the front, feeling creepier still, half convinced I would find the claybank gone or maybe dead with his throat cut.

He was there on dropped reins just like I had left him and ears cocked, watching me, blew through his nose a soft whicker, like relief.

I gave him a pat and tramped back through the house finding everything ship-shape. No sign of a struggle, no bullet holes, nothing to suggest what had happened to these people.

It was enough, by grab, to make anyone jumpy.

There'd been clothes in the bunkhouse and, in the front room here, an open book folded over a chair arm — Tierlanno's *Irrigation* — like a man might leave it if he'd been called to the door.

Considerable puzzled and not a little mistrustful, I took the lamp into the bedroom for another look around. I went through the drawers, found a town suit in the closet and begun to put together a faceless picture of what the guy looked like. On the short side, probably five foot four or five by the clothes and spare, likely wiry. The boots standing under the suit were Hyers, hand stitched, with stars on the uppers and a gouge on one heel that didn't look too recent. Three of the white shirts in the drawers had ruffles down the front like a gambler's, and there was two pairs of sleeve garters, colorful enough to have come off the legs of some dancehall queen. Bit of a dude, I thought, peering.

Recollecting my horse I took him round to the barn, filling a battered bucket from a pump outside the open front door. I shucked off my gear and hazed him into a stall after giving the place a hasty onceover in the light of a match before shaking down a couple armfuls of hay. And, since I figured to spend what was left of the night here, I took the precaution of fastening him in.

To tell the plain truth, I didn't noways cotton to the idea of staying in so vulnerable a position. I'd been intending to ride on, but this situation begged a closer inspection in the full light of day and I figured I ought to see it in the same shape I'd found it. If there was tracks I didn't want to find them rubbed out. Particular around the front of that house.

Back in the big room, feeling some conspicuous, I yanked down the shades. Then, carrying the lamp, I went over to the desk. The rolled top of it was locked, but one of the drawers hadn't quite clicked shut. There wasn't nothing in it to identify the owner. Finding out who he was likely wouldn't help much, but this whole deal looked so uncommon strange I figured to sleep better if I knew.

I started back towards the bedroom and that closet hung suit. There might be something in the pockets — a letter was what I had in mind. But on my way to the door my glance fell again across the sprawled-open book. Without clear purpose I picked it up, riffled the pages without reward. Then I thought to look in the front of it.

Across the inside of the cover, boldly written in blue ink, was two words that hit me like a swung fist: *Fletcher Dowling.*

I must of gaped like a ninny.

All kind of wild notions struck up a quiver, but even through this avalanche of thinking I'd no trouble recollecting where I'd last heard that name nor the way them words had been flung at me. It all come back like pieces of blown-off roof dropping round.

I could see that bug-eyed barkeep staring, the smoldery look of Pot Gut tugging and the twisted-round hateful honey sweet sneer of Taffy Hair crying: *"Whyn't you try Fletch Dowlin'?"*

Some things a guy does without even knowing. It was this way when I blew out the lamp to stand there stiff and crouched in the blackness, not breathing, mouth open to catch the faintest scrape of sound.

Only thing I could hear was the jerky wheezing thump of my heart.

I didn't get much sleep in Dowling's bed what with rolling and tossing the biggest part of the night. I come full awake and bolt upright twenty times I guess with the sweat pouring out of me, gun fisted, every nerve ajangle.

When I ought to have awake I was pounding my ear, sawing logs like some drunk after a three-day toot. First I knowed things was not the way I'd left them was when I opened hurting eyes to find the place sun lit and full of glowering strangers.

Must of been six anyways crowding round the foot of the bed, fanned out hostile behind a puckerjawed dame with sorghum colored eyes that — to my notion anyhow — looked riled as a she-tiger hunting lost cubs.

Being woke this way in nothing but long-handles ain't the kind of thing I'd recommend to no one. I was fixing to grab up the blankets some nump had pulled off when a grip like a vise latched onto my arm.

"Easy, Mack — *easy,*" someone growled in my ear. "Don't try on nothin' reckless without you're bustin' to raise a few humps."

Like dry sticks snapping this female says, "What's your name?"

"Chrissake, lady, lemme get on some clothes!"

Her look didn't change but I see her eyes swivel. "Dump that bucket."

I yelled, "Creepin' Moses!" when that cold water hit. I come out of that right into his arms and it was like being grabbed by a goddam grizzly. All the air whooshed out of me. I quit struggling pronto.

He let up a little.

"What's your name?" She said it again and he give me a squeeze just to let me know he was still there and able.

"Adams," I gasped — "Pearly Adams," and gulped, reaching deep for enough breath to float it. "Will somebody tell me —"

"Turn him loose, Curly."

His hair, horsetail brown, was straight as a Injun's.

"Now suppose you tell us," she said in clipped tones, "what you're doing here, Adams."

"Just passin' through."

Curly flexed his fingers and grinned. "All who believes that can stand on their head." He looked for a sign. "You want I should bend this jigger a mite?"

Her voice said to me, "And you just happened to see this nice empty house and —"

"It wasn't that way at all," I growled, and felt Curly, restless like, kneading his biceps.

But I was commencing to take in more of this now. Good enough that I could see — despite the fact she had on her paw's pants — this was just a dang girl being so flip with her chin music; she looked like being even younger than I was.

It was powerful apparent she didn't have much sense, because no decent female that was in her right mind would ever climb into no getup like that.

I said, fishing for something that might sound like the truth, "As a matter of fact —"

61

"Never mind stringin' together no lies. You're a caught fence crawler no matter what else." Her eyes swiveled round, then come back at me grimly. "I suppose you're ridin' for Hard Nose Hank." She curled her lip. "You can read, can't you?"

"Do I look like a idjit?"

"That about sums it up." She peered at me nastily. "You couldn't *be* on this spread without knowing it was posted."

"I saw a sign," I admitted, "but —"

"You come right ahead anyway."

"Figures," Curly said, and some of them others nodded.

I couldn't seem to lay hold of nothing likely enough to put into words. The feel of this deal was getting worse by the minute — seemed like out of all proportion to the size of what I'd done. Way that bunch was eyeing me was too damned ugly to contemplate.

"Buck," Curly said, "fetch in that rope off my saddle."

CHAPTER 7

My throat got drier than an empty tub.

If I hadn't been where I was I'd never of believed it for a minute. Hanging a guy for trespass was just plain downright loco, but this bunch, by the look, was plenty crazy enough to do it. That girl hadn't even turned a hair.

The guy he had spoke to left the foot of the bed and the drag of rowels went off towards the porch. I heard a door slam.

The girl's watching eyes looked hard as creek stones.

Cold sweat broke through the frozen stillness of my skin and the stillness all around so filled with glowering looks was suddenly more than I could stand. "Now see here!" I rasped, knocking Curly's hand away; and right about then that feller, Buck, come back with the rope.

"You got any last words," Curly said, "hang onto 'em. You kin speak your piece when you're under that tree. Climb into your clothes," he growled, stepping back, eager to embrace anything I might try. He hadn't even bothered to put a gun on me though mine was dangling from its belt in one hand.

That girl was large on the horizon of my thoughts as I scrootched around to stomp into my boots. I felt downright meachin, some furious too as, nagged by worries, I sloshed into my hat. I had to get up to catch hold of my pants but with them buckled around me I began to take note of a number of things.

What give her the right to make like Moses? If Dowling was married I'd seen nothing to show it. I got into my shirt. "You Dowlin's daughter?"

The air tightened up. It was Curly that answered. "How'd you know Dowlin' *had* a daughter?" And the Buck with the scowl of a bloodhound wanted to know how Dowling got into this confab.

Looked like I'd put both feet plumb into it.

An obvious stranger, they had hit on the notion I was here in the pay of some obstreperous character she'd called Hard Nose Hank, and this tossing of Dowling's name into the pot had not noticeably endeared me none. I sure wasn't thinking like one of Cap's boys, but I could see plain enough I'd got to do some tall talking. Dowling's name had not been on that sign. The point wasn't whether she was Dowling's daughter, but how had I known about him in the first place?

Stuffing shirttails into my pants, and some flustered, I sneaked a look at the girl, found her rummaging my face with that clawhammer stare. "So I made a bum guess," I grunted at Curly. "Nothin' strange about that — I only come into this neighborhood yesterday. Guess I musta stepped out the wrong side of my blanket."

Nobody spoke. I saw no change in their faces.

Grabbing breath I said doggedly, "I been seein' some country. Run out of smokin'. Yesterday, at Charleston, I stopped off at Scott's to get me some Durham. While I was there some hardcase come in an' asked the girl where her old man was, an' right away started getting unpleasant. I put a fist in his face and he banged into the shelvin'. A can of bully beef fell on his head. The girl run. Seemed kind of smart for me to sift along likewise. Which I done, ridin' the river."

Then I told about that business at the

road ranch — all of it, caught some knowing looks at the part about Dowling. "So I
pushed on," I said, "an' come to this fence.
It was night pretty near. My belly was
growling and I figured I could anyways get
directions. I followed it west and come in
through a gate —"

"That was padlocked."

"Yeah. I shot the lock off. I shouted a few
times when I come into the yard. Since I
got no answer I went through the buildin's.
There was nobody round. Seemed odd —
I'd thought at least to find coosie."

"So you made yourself at home."

"Custom of the country —"

"To sleep in the owner's bed?" Curly said.

"I stayed in the house because I wanted,
soon's it was light, to have a look round for
tracks. The whole thing struck me as uncommon queer. As for knowin' who owned
the place, I found his name in a book folded
over a chair arm."

"Nothin' like having the run of the
house!"

That was one of them others. All their
looks was on me and they all looked the
same now. I could tell how the skunk felt at
Hildebrandt's box social. Even the tops of
my ears turned hot.

"I'm tellin' you how it was!" I scowled.

66

"What would the likes of *you* have done, steered into this kinda setup? When I come onto that name I couldn't of figured out up from down! Believe me I was scairt plumb silly —"

"But not scared enough to light a shuck."

That was Curly again, still using my cartridge belt for an anchor. I couldn't tell what he thought from his face. He was put together on about the same scale as that feller in town the beef had fell on. "Most guys in a bind like that would of dived for their saddle, made far apart tracks." It looked like he was weighing me over. "This gazabo in town you claim was botherin' Connie — the girl at Scott's — you catch his name?"

I shook my head.

"Big," I said, "kinda built like you. Tobacco chewer — never cared none where he chucked his spit. Batwing chaps. Wore a black wool shirt and cowhide vest . . ."

I was stopped by a flood of disbelieving stares. He didn't call me a liar; there was nothing on his face at all. He kept watching sharp as a cat at a mousehole. "Anything else you can remember about him?"

"Called me 'sport' . . . if that helps any. Guess that's the size of it."

Them cow nurses back of the girl swapped

looks and there was nothing about it that boded me good.

Curly hefted my shell belt. "A real cute yarn —"

Buck's snort, loud and ugly, rode through his words. "Any chump with his eyes shut could describe his own boss!"

And the girl said, stormy eyed, "How much did they hand you to squat on this spread?"

It looked an extra good place to catch hold of my temper. I said quiet, "I wasn't squattin'. An' all I ever been handed is trouble! That jigger in town —"

"Call him Hard Nose Hank. At least that's the handle of the ranny you described. Lockhart's pet *mover!*"

I had halfway suspected it. Searching their faces I didn't see much to hope for. "That's not my fault — I can't help how it looks. I told you the straight of it!" Grinding my teeth I yelled in a fury. "First I ever laid eyes on the cold mouthed lobster was where he come in an' started maulin' the kid. I grabbed a fistful of collar, smacked him into them shelves —"

"That," Curly said, "is the part I can't swaller. A half pint like you tyin' into that gunny, knockin' him hell west and crooked."

"It was a *can* done that!" I raked them

68

with despairing eyes. "I told — God damn it, the can's right out there on my saddle!"

"Buck, take a look," the girl said, halfway believing. But before he even got out of his tracks Curly growled, "What'll that prove? Of course he's got a can on his rig! Whole deal's been tailored to fit what he told us, even to that pair he run into at Bolton's — the ones, I mean, he claims to've run into. Lockhart never does anything by halves."

Her stare came back, darkening, trying I suppose to figure out what I was like, if I was wild enough maybe to of had any hand in whatever it was had happened to Dowling. I don't know what she saw but I got to admit that for a filly she was pert enough. Or would of been, dressed right. Good strong jaw. Hair like a vulture's wing. Teeth that was whiter than a new deck of cards. And them brown eyes of hers could really get into you.

"All right. We'll *all* take a squint," Curly muttered, disgusted. He growled over his shoulder as he headed for the yard, "Couple of you fetch along His Nibs, the giant slayer. An' keep your eyes peeled sharp for tricks."

With one guy anchored to each of my arms I had to go along whether I cottoned to it or not, him and her walking half a rope's length ahead. I could see him jawing

69

at her clean to the barn.

I didn't think that can was going to help me a heap. Because — like he'd said — what the hell did it prove except I'd stopped at Scott's store? I couldn't even feel sure it was any proof of that.

But when I got inside with the rest of them crowded round and Curly, mean mouthed, said, "Let's see it," I knew any good it might of done was up the creek. For I could see as well of them before I even put my hand up there was no can inside that rolled slicker.

CHAPTER 8

I didn't bother to touch it.

What the hell was the use? Any nump could see nothing big enough to clobber a guy was hid inside the folds of that fish. Without *that* there was nothing at all I could offer in support of the barest part of my yarn. Except the badge of an Arizona Ranger.

Once I chucked that into the pot I'd be no more use in this country to Mossman than a .22 cartridge in a eight-gauge gun.

First off I figured one of these scowlers had lifted it, but that didn't make too much sense either. I'd probably lost it somewheres back along the trail. Cussing wouldn't help. I looked up at Curly and, tight mouthed, shrugged.

"Ain't run outa words, have you?" His eyes turned sardonic. "Didn't think for a minute lack of that can would be anything to throw a man of your imagination."

Feller might as well argue with the shadow of death.

Getting no rise out of me didn't bother him. He tipped his head, grinning, at the pair hanging onto me. "Put him under a tree. Buck, git his horse." His eyes was wicked.

But the girl cried: "Wait!"

They all turned to look.

Like a practiced skater going over thin ice she said, "You could be wrong. About him."

She sounded — I was going to say nervous, but it was more like uncertain.

Curly said with a graveling forbearance, "We been all over this. You know what's at stake —"

"But we don't have to *kill* him."

Curly rolled up his eyes. "He is kinda young, I got to admit. An' not bad lookin'. But snakes come in all sizes an' some of the littlest is the worst to git hit by." He jerked a nod at the pair that had hold of me.

She put out a hand, dark eyes going darker. "I won't have it. Turn him loose."

"Now wait a minute," Curly growled, looking testy. His worth in his job with the crew was at stake. He beckoned her aside but the girl never budged; apparently she counted a man's life more important.

I didn't figure it was me, more the principle of the thing that had put her back up. Her stubborn opposition only settled his convictions; you could see the outraged boil of resentment in the thrust of his jaw.

She didn't back off though her eyes were big. "Turn him loose."

"Then you got a choice. Him or me!"

She chewed at her lip. She had pride, too, and right on her side, but you could tell the threat of losing him scared her. Likely almost as much as seeing me swung.

Cold drops of sweat run down my back. I was bracing myself for what I figured was certain when she said, looking hard at him, "If I didn't always have to be dealing with *men* I think I could take all the rest of it in stride."

He peered at her huffily. "What's that supposed t' mean?"

"There must be a better way than tearing headlong into the face of every challenge!"

"All right." He spoke through twisted lips. "You go ahead an' name it, missy."

"Don't give me that! This isn't marbles or chalk. You can't give a man back his *life* if you're wrong!"

Curly looked his contempt.

"It's that kinda mamby-pamby slop that's give those bastards the jump in the first place. Your ol' man was strong fer that guff too an' what did it git him? A hole in the ground!"

"Dad was killed by a *horse.* You heard the verdict —"

"A 'accident.' Sure." It came sour off his tongue. "An' that money he borrored you never knew nothin' about." He smashed the hat against his leg, intolerance corrugating his jowls. "A nice thing for Lockhart — an' we'll git more of the same when they fetch in Fletch Dowlin'! You're gonna git smashed if you don't take steps!"

"I'll be smashed a lot worse if we start taking wrong ones."

Confused and upset by the loss of old values she was still, I thought, trying desperately to grasp how violence had come to be the only thing men respected. She seemed to search his face without benefit. "I suppose . . ." she said, and let it go. "Perhaps you're right about Lockhart's intentions —"

"You ain't *blind!* The guy's already grabbed half this county! You think he'll pass up —"

"He isn't God. He's not behind every bush."

"Well, he's back of enough. Him and his understrappers — an' every dirty deal that's been hatched around here you kin bet he's got a finger in! A syndicate shyster sent in t' take over —"

74

"You make him sound . . . Oh, Curly!" she cried, throwing out both hands, "can't you see he's a man, not some unfeeling avalanche? He can laugh, he can cry. He's just as human as we are. He can make mistakes, too, and he can be stopped —"

"By a bullet. Sure. But there ain't nothin' else gonna stop that bastard. You better believe it."

I cleared my throat. It whipped both their heads around.

"Adams," she said, "I think you've told us the truth. If I turn you loose will you ride off and stay out of this?"

"Well . . ." I scuffed a boot, uneasy with Curly's scowl stabbing at me. "I've got to find work, ma'am —"

"Do you think Hard Nose Hank, that man you interfered with back in town, will let you stay?"

"I can take care of myself," I said, flushing at the unexpected loudness of my words.

Curly just stood there hefting my shell belt, sandy jowls unreadable, eyes half shut.

She darted a glance at him, nervous and showing it in the way her tongue licked across dry lips.

"Go ahead," Curly growled. "We could use another hand. Put him on if you wanta."

She stared, open mouthed, while he tossed

the belt at me. Their hands fell away and I scooped it up, went after the jarred-loose gun, feeling his look as I upended the barrel.

The muzzle seemed clean enough, no grit clogged its snout. I dropped it into its holster, flipped the belt round me and took up the slack, just leaving enough to let it sag proper.

She said, "Where are you going?" in a half frightened bleat.

He was turning away but his eyes come back, crossing my face like the touch of cold fingers. "Not far enough t' let you git into trouble." He let out a snort and went stomping off.

CHAPTER 9

Seemed like we both felt a mite uneasy — I sure did with them eyes flickering over me, the silence thick enough to stab with a knife.

It was hard not to feel this turnabout on his part went considerable deeper than appeared on the surface. He wasn't the kind to swap a horse in mid channel.

So why had he practically *told* her to hire me? To make sure I was where he could keep a eye on me? Guide my hand to his own ends, maybe? To have me where he could settle my hash if it turned out that was what he wanted to do?

I'd be lying if I told you it was no skin off my nose. It could be the whole nose if I didn't look sharp. But one way I was satisfied. Any joker grim as him would sure as hell never be far from the action!

I peered at the girl again, swapping stares with her, wondering about a whole heap of things. Her old man — if he'd been killed by a horse or some devilment of Lockhart's — couldn't very well be the missing Fletch Dowling.

"Mebbe," I said, "you better fill me in." With her hands shoved in gloves the way they was, I couldn't tell if she had a ring on or not. Seemed there had to be some connection. "If you're Missus Dowlin' —"

"I'm not 'missus' anyone," she said like she needed another man in her life just a little bit less than she did three ears or a hydrophoby skunk. "I'm Belulah Bandle — Belle for short."

I grimaced. "Pleased t' meet you." It came out stiff as a broom handle, which it generally does when I stray from the truth. But no one noticed, I reckon, because just then Buck wanted to know if he should wave in the boys with the horses.

Only horse stock I could see, looking round, was them flyswishing saddlers this bunch had come on.

Our eyes met again. When she didn't straightoff give the feller an answer he growled, impatient: "We're still movin' in, ain't we?"

She could tell by my face when my wits got to working. She cried, "Well — what about it? If *we* don't *he* will!"

Him being so much in my mind I thought

first off she meant Curly, which didn't make sense; then I see she meant Lockhart — his mover, maybe. Time I got that much un-scrambled she was telling Buck: "Go ahead. Call 'em in."

"Two wrongs," I said, "don't make it right."

The look this fetched was hard to swal-low, a three way cross that twisted her mouth. Pity was there and plain contempt, but plainest of all was indignation. It come out of those eyes like sparks.

"For your information —" she hauled a deep breath — "I *own* this spread!"

Quite a fistful of things bolted through my head. This was no piddlin' outfit — best grass I had seen. What few cows I'd got near enough to read had packed Walking M brands and the name on that sign — that irrigation book too! — had been sure as hell *Dowling.* I told her as much and got a withering sniff.

"Fletch had the place under lease, but — Why should I stand here arguin' with you!" she cried, exasperated, eyes full of anger. "If you want a job go lend a hand with them horses. If you don't you better make tracks while you're able."

I hadn't played this too well, not even by

ear, and as the day wore along it was plain by the looks of what hands I rubbed up against, I was here under sufferance. I wasn't let to forget it.

Guards was put out but I wasn't one of them. I slept in the bunkhouse and ate with the crew. With, but not of. Sour looks made that plain enough.

Two days passed, bright with the glare of midsummer heat. Curly kept half the crew riding fence. No trouble developed that anyone could notice. The fence wasn't breached, no strangers was sighted. Whatever had taken Dowling away from this spread hadn't been content to stop with him and his crew; there wasn't enough of his cattle left to fill a corral. Had he driven them off or had someone else got them?

On the third morning when I stepped out to wash up, there was cattle all over — *her* cows. Straddlebug branded.

I suppose it made sense; she could hardly afford a working crew at both places. Even if she could find enough hands.

After I'd tossed my plate in the wreck pan and Curly had laid out the work for the rest of them, he beckoned me aside. "Man I sent off to check your story got back."

"So I told you the truth."

He give me the benefit of that unwinking

stare. "Don't stand too free. Only sign of you ever bein' in Charleston was a guy who claimed to've seen some jigger ridin' your color of hoss headin' north up the river 'bout an hour after sunup. He wasn't even sure which mornin' it was."

"How about the girl?"

"Girl's gone. Her ol' man's dead. Fished him out of a hole — broken neck. Scott's place is padlocked. Sign on the door says 'Gone to Texas.' "

"What about that road ranch?"

"Couldn't git a thing outa Bolton. Wouldn't admit you was there; never seen that pair you described; never heard of 'em."

It figured. Every bit of it. Not all of the Know Nothings was gone from the land. Round Charleston these days I guessed it could be a pretty popular creed.

"What do you expect me to say?"

His eyes dug into me, sharp as stone splinters. "You watch yourself. I've still got this rope and it'll work just as good from the back of a hoss. Now git back to your screw worms."

I done considerable thinking as I went about my chores. Didn't seem like being here was going to get me much forwarder with what had fetched me into this country. Too much distrust hanging over this spread

81

and over me in particular. I didn't have to have my palm read to know I was being watched. It crossed my mind I might do better in town.

But that night when I rode in, I could sense a change no more than I climbed out of my saddle. Two of the guys even nodded in a kind of grudging fashion. All through supper there was more and freer talk. Several things was passed to me with "Hev some more of this?" And three different times I was asked for an opinion.

When the crew, getting out their makings, filed out to squat and shoot the breeze, Curly, lingering at the door, looked back at me and, snorting, said: "You're not out of the woods yet, Adams."

But, after he had gone, Coosie met my look with a wink and a chuckle.

And, outside, the others made room for me, Wishbone tossing me his sack of Durham. As I shaped up a smoke someone found a lighted match.

Looked like I was being taken into the tribe, but I wasn't so overjoyed I passed up the notion this was some kind of trick. Not figuring to stick my jaw out none I dropped down beside Wishbone, returning his sack. He was older than the rest. Maybe he figured he could afford to be neighborly.

He was a bowlegged gander with a face more carved up by wrinkles than a prune. But it was Buck who said, "Tell us again about that can clobberin' Hank. Did it sure 'nough flatten him? What'd he say when he rejoined the quick?"

I said, "I thought you waddies was afraid of poison oak."

"Aw, that was Curly," Buck said. "He's got a suspicious nature — has t' sneak up on the dipper just t' git hisself a drink. Anyway, we know different now."

And Wishbone told me, "Bert Klingerman was by — his land joins ours off beyond them windcut buttes. Said he'd seen Hank in town with a swole-up jaw an' a rag round his noggin. Said it looked like the sorry puke was gunnin' fer bear — you wanta watch yourself."

"Wa'n't you scairt?" someone asked.

I said I reckoned I hadn't known enough to be till after I'd tied into him. "Soon's I had me a chance to get a good look at him I rattled my hocks an' got out of there pronto."

A laugh went round. "He's a mean one," Buck said. "He don't no more worry about unlimberin' that gun than one of Mamie's girls would of peelin' bare nakid."

"Where does Mamie's girls perform?" I

asked and, after the hooting that followed, Wishbone said serious, "You better steer clear of town till that hombre cools off."

CHAPTER 10

Biggest thing wrong with most good advice is the guy it's scraped up for generally can't or won't take it.

Brother, I been there.

Long after the relief had rode off to their whack at patroling the fence, and the rest had turned in, I stuck to the shadows of the mess shack wall trying to figure some way of getting clear of this outfit long enough to take just such a pasear.

The hazards of this did not completely escape me — I wasn't as big a fool as you might reasonably think. I might not have been quite dry behind the ears, but I had been weaned and reckoned to hold my own in most company.

The chance of running into Lockhart's mover was an ever present threat, but I couldn't believe he was being paid to waste much time in the bars of Charleston.

Straddlebug, if the girl really owned it,

had plenty of reason to move onto this spread, and even more reason to look for trouble on account of it. So why was the syndicate fooling around? Why weren't they over here, lock, stock and fireworks?

In Lockhart's boots a guy was bound to be cagey, but that was no answer. I needed a fresh line on this, a wider sampling of public opinion than I was likely to get ridding bovines of screw worms. A better slant on Lockhart's tactics; a chance, if possible, to size him up. Even if he'd no connection with whatever had happened to Dowling and his outfit, it just wasn't natural a jigger paid to expand would let this kind of setup go by default.

I wondered what Belulah found to do with her evenings. Reading, probably — I couldn't see but one light.

I had a wild thought then. What if Lockhart hadn't set this up? Supposing Dowling's trouble was the work of this guy Curly. . . .

But I shook my head, I couldn't see no good way he could profit. A range feud, of course, could be pretty good insurance for wholesale thievery. Fortunes had been built on just such a dido in Texas — all over, but Belle Bandle's range boss couldn't be crammed into that kind of caper. Not in *my* mind. I couldn't believe he had the patience or inventiveness. He fit better the picture I had pieced together of Lockhart. Ruthless, driving, steamrolling force.

Grinding the butt of my smoke into the dirt, I chanced to glance toward the house as I started to push up, saw the shape of a man briefly caught against the narrowing oblong of a soundlessly shut door.

Coosie said in the grunt of a whisper, "Just business, kid. Whatever you're thinkin' git it outa your head."

I was reminded of the 'business' Lockhart's mover had with Connie.

Next morning before I'd got up from my breakfast or had chance to call for a second cup of java, one of the faster stuffers come in from the yard with word I was wanted up at the house.

I peered at Curly, saw his mouth pull down, but there was nothing to be read from the flats of his stare. He didn't say nothing, neither, so I got up and went out.

It was him I'd seen quit the house last night when Coosie, mumbling caution, had come up out of the dark.

I reached for the makings as I crossed the yard, had a smoke shaped and burning time I hit the porch. I put a thump of knuckles against the paintless door, conscious of eyes boring into the parts of me that couldn't look back.

Her voice, sounding muffled, called, "In here, Adams."

With a final drag I flipped the coffin nail onto bare ground, hauled open the door with a scoop of the hand and — with considerable less assurance than I would like to of felt — set off through the house.

She was in the front room, bent over the desk with the top of it open and a scowl in the look she threw over one shoulder. "When you were being so free in this place did you see any ledgers or account books around?"

Being alone like this with her inside four walls was a mighty pale carbon to what the prospect had offered. I was too mixed up to do more than shake my head.

"I can't find even a tally," she grumbled and, scowl deepening, chewed a while on her lip. Then she put it aside. Straightening, looking square at me, she said, "I want you to go into town for me, Adams. I've some things coming in on the stage you're to fetch."

I considered her a spell, saw her cheek color changing. I said, "What about Curly?"

"Where does he fit into this?"

"Well . . ." I said, shifting under the search of her stare. "Ain't he like to have somethin' else planned for me to do?"

Her mouth tightened up. "Let's get this straight, Adams, once and for all. The Straddlebug payroll comes out of my pocket."

"I ain't arguin' with that. It's just — when you hire a segundo, he expects to give the orders. A spread with two bosses —"

"You trying to tell me how to manage my affairs?"

"No, ma'am," I said, and should have quit right there. I had no hugs for Curly, but right is right and I told her so. "You're weakenin' his hold on the crew. No matter what you want done it oughta come through —"

"Are you refusing to go into town on this errand?"

With her chin up that way, all her feathers rumpled, she was something to see. I shifted uncomfortably. "*Are* you?" she cried.

I said, "I'll check with the boss —"

"Just a minute!" she snapped, yanking me around. "I'm not done with you yet!" We swapped cat and dog glares. Suddenly she broke out a grin. "You've certainly got your . . . How did you get to be so insufferable?"

When I didn't say nothing she continued

89

to peer. Halfway, it seemed, between outrage and laughter. "Nothing you do makes a damned bit of sense!" She eyed me some more. "Don't you care if you're fired?"

"Not a heap," I said, as she looked her astonishment, "I never thought to be ridin' for no petticoat spread."

"Kind of young for a woman hater, aren't you? All right." She shook her head. "Get Curly's blessing. Here — you'll need this." She thrust a rumple of bills at me.

Goldbacks.

Without counting I stuffed them into a shirt pocket, clapped on my hat and got the hell out of there.

I found Curly lounging in the mess shack door. He listened to my story, shrugged, spat and snorted. "What the hell you waitin' on?" Without another glance he climbed into his saddle and jogged off after the departing crew.

Coosie stepped to the door as I swung toward the barn. "You watch your step, boy," he growled, looking hard at me.

All the way into town — I took the wagon road this time — it kept running through my head there must be something more behind this than what had been spread out for me to goggle at. With Curly swinging a

90

sharp eye for trouble, it didn't make sense I'd be sent into town for anything at all without his approval. It had, I figured, to be a test of some kind. With me, easiest spared, on the baited end. And seemed like the cook must of had the same notion.

The chance I'd figured to make to see Lockhart began, even to me, to appear kind of out of focus. No guy suspicious as Curly was going to let me ride into town un-watched. Maybe, I thought, that there was the nub of it, the whole thing cooked up to observe what I might do with an apparent opportunity for unrestricted movement.

It began to seem like I had wasted my concern over the rights of that cold-jawed whippoorwill. Way things was shaping, I wouldn't of put it past him to have sparked the whole deal.

This wagon road, cutting straight across the flats, must have shortened the distance by ten or twelve miles. It missed the tumble-down road ranch complete. Only twice did I even catch glimpses of the river. Charles-ton hove into sight something less than quarter of an hour after straight-up noon.

First ranny I hailed told me where to find the stage office. Three blocks down I was still, in spite of everything, toying with the notion of looking up Lockhart when, on a building just past the Wells Fargo office, a twelve-foot sign drew my eye: TWO-POLE PUMPKIN LAND & CATTLE COMPANY — Dallas Lockhart, Dist. Mgr.

If you think that set me back, you're right.

But it was nothing to the nerve-thumping jolt I got when, having dismounted in front of the stage office, I saw across the top of my saddle the last guy I wanted any truck with right then.

Hard Nose Hank — and he was coming straight at me!

CHAPTER 11

The son of a bitch wasn't gnashing no teeth.

With a snake or a redskin a guy pretty generally knows where he's at. A trouble-huntin' Injun puts on paint. Snakes rattle. All Lockhart's mover showed above the collar was a grin that reached from here to there.

I sure didn't know whether to jump or run.

There was things I could of done, I expect, if they had crossed my mind. Time they did it was already too late. All that traffic — every jigger in sight — come complete to a standstill.

My legs was cold clean down to my boot-soles.

"Well, well!" he chortled, stepping round my horse, all his dog teeth showing. "If it ain't my old friend Slap-an'-Run Sammy!"

There wasn't no place I could get to beat a bullet.

I had to try several times before I could get words to talk with. Then they come in a rush too fast to sort. Too goddam loud I heard myself saying: "Ain't you found no girls to rip the clothes off of this mornin'?"

The grin flaked off his ugly teeth, lips showing blue along the gash of his mouth. The whole top half of him shivered and swelled. One hand jumped for leather as he bent from the waist. I didn't wait round for no plainer intention.

I grabbed at bone handles in a sweat of cold horror.

You know how it is in a nightmare? I died, I think, a dozen deaths before the feel of them fit my hand. I thought that rod never would come free, wondering why the damn fool didn't fire.

The racket and bang of it smashed against buildings, the sounds dropping off like pieces of glass. Two-thirds of his gun was still deep in its holster so it had to be me that had got off that shot. It was plain I had missed. A .44 slug don't leave room for much doubt and he was still on his feet.

A gout of cloth, then, no bigger than a dime, fell out of his sleeve just above the wrist and slithered groundward, light and slow as a feather. I heard the gasps that come out of dry thoats. But I could breathe again.

His eyes looked like they would roll off his cheekbones.

I caught up with myself, pushed my iron back in leather like I didn't, by God, care if school kept or not. I was turning away, fixing to catch up my reins, when a rusty voice called. "Here! You there — come up here!"

It come from the porch of that place next door, the one with the syndicate's sign on the roof. I guess you know I was pleased with myself. "Old man," I said, "was you talkin' at me?"

He inclined his head, waxy glance unreadable.

I had him pegged, though he wasn't quite what I'd expected of Lockhart. No Johnny Bull type — he didn't even look Texican. More the kind of Kentucky colonel you see in the ads for high-proof whiskey. But I wasn't afraid of him. In my rough drifter's clothes, pulling my fidgeting horse along behind, I stepped up to the porch rail, giving back stare for stare.

"What do you want?"

The shock of caught breaths was sweet as old wine.

He considered me, not speaking, for half a dozen heart thumps — time enough, he

95

probably thought, to set a fast gun into proper perspective.

Unabashed I stood waiting. I had all the time in the world right then.

It was him that finally swiveled his glance. It fetched Hank, flushed and dragfooted over. "Ponchatraine," he said, "what was that all about?"

Hank's bull neck turned darker and thicker. "Happens every day — you oughta know how it is."

"Suppose you tell me."

"A man gets a rep, every snotnose kid in the country wants t' take him on just t' show how goddam tough they are!"

He sloshed the chew around with his jaws, chucked me a murderous look and spat. "You don't think this kid had me *buffaloed* do you?" He said through his teeth, "I coulda cut him in half before his iron —"

"No need to pretend with me," I laughed. "Any time you feel lucky you know what to do."

That was hitting him hard right where he lived. But it was crowd him, I thought, or wind up dead in some alley. I wanted it now while I had him in front of me.

Most guys in his place with half the town looking on would of figured there hadn't been no choice left, but all he done was scowl and look nasty.

I said loud and clear: "Reckon you'd liefer keep on being a live coward with a stripe up your back than risk your luck while a man's lookin' at you."

He carried it off a heap better than I'd looked for. "See?" he cried, wheeling back to his boss with outflung arms. "They'll do anythin' t' goad a fast gun into drawin' — *anything!*"

It was good enough I guessed to fool a lot of this crowd. It might of fooled Lockhart — no way for me to tell. Chewing at his mustache the Two-Pole Pumpkin boss, thoughtful like, nodded. "You'd better get that vented stuff moved straight away," he grunted, dismissing him.

Then he peered at me. "What did you say your name was?"

"It's Adams," I said, hoping the shake in my knees wasn't obvious.

"Looks like you got away with the brass ring. You always so reckless in your dealings with strangers?"

"That polecat wasn't no stranger to me. I caught him maulin' that girl at Scott's store the other mornin' and —"

Lockhart held up a hand. Concerned, he said, "I'd like to hear more about that — matter of fact; the girl's disappeared. They fished her father out of a prospect hole yesterday morning with a broken neck."

Nibbling his mustache he considered me intently. "Tell you what . . . Why don't you drop out to my place in a little bit? We can discuss this over a bait of lunch. . . ." He must of seen from my face I wasn't hugging the notion. He threw me a smile. "You're not afraid of me, are you?"

"What's to be afraid of?" I said, bristling.

"Then I'll expect you." He nodded. "You might even find it profitable. Make it one o'clock. Won't take you over five minutes." And before I could open my mouth he was gone.

The rest of the crowd begun to break away, too.

I caught a brief glimpse of Wishbone, but he slipped away before I could get at him. The old coot was probably bird-dogging for Curly. Pushing him out of my thoughts, I went into the stage office. Asked if they had anything for Straddlebug.

"Got a parcel here I been holdin' for Miz Belle," the clerk said, fetching it. I took it out, tied it back of my saddle, a pretty flimsy business for so much bother. Recollecting I was supposed to pay for it, I went back. Took all the money she'd give me.

"Dresses," the clerk winked. "They come high."

I see by the clock it was ten to one. "Which way do I go to find Lockhart's house?"

He stopped dead, looking queer, then pulled me over to the door. "Big white one — right up there," he pointed, and stood a spell, staring, like he figured all the monkeys wasn't at the zoo yet.

I wasn't so sure, by grab, he was wrong. But I climbed aboard Old Snuffy, my claybank, and pointed him up the hill just the same. I doubted I would find out anything useful but it was a lead-pipe cinch I wouldn't be staying away. And there was always the chance folks had the wrong slant on this resident manager. Be worth something to get to the straight of that.

Which fetched my thoughts circling back to Hank. I could picture him easy and knew I had better keep my eyes skun sharp. No bullet ever gave a damn whose name was on it.

Lockhart's white house was enclosed in a picket fence, high and sharp enough to keep cattle off it. The yard inside was bright with flowers.

Leaving my mount on trailing reins near enough to switch flies with the manager's roan, I let myself through, climbed the porch steps and knocked.

Brisk sounds tapped out an imminent approach. Figured to be a female, and I had just about time to drag the hat off my head when I found her confronting me through the stretched mesh of the door's new screen. Reckon I gaped like a ninny.

She pushed open the door. "You must be Mr. Adams," she said, and all I could do was gulp, staring tongue-tied.

She had a frilly little apron tied round the front of her, but it wasn't the apron that had me goggling. She was the most female female I had ever clamped eyes on. Hell, I hadn't even known they built them like her!

Reasonable tall she was, but a heap on the puny side — 'delicate,' I expect, is what you'd call her, so chalk-white pale I figured she was about to come down with a swoon or had someway tangled with a dose of rat-killer.

I could see blue veins on the back of her hands, and the thump of her heart every time she drew breath made the bulge-puckered top of her waist kind of wriggle. Nothing ornery in my head, but she spotted me watching. My cheeks got hot enough to fry eggs and bacon.

She kind of flushed a little, too, but you

could tell she was a sure enough lady. Her mouth didn't tighten; she never pulled up her chin or made any motions to yelp for help. Just kept looking with them big horsey eyes that was like two pansies in the garden of her face.

Put me six steps lower than the belly of a snake. I'd of sooner been nabbed trying to make off with the Christmas Orphans Fund, and me a new deacon.

I can't tell you yet if her eyes were blue, green or brown. Her hair though, piled up on top of her head, was bright as a halo of rust colored gold, like a helmet fresh shined. And her voice — it was like the tinkling of tiny chimes reaching out across a valley of knee-deep grass. She looked — never mind the apron — about as dewy eyed and helpless as a new dropped foal.

Gulping, I admitted to being Pearly Adams. "Mister Lockhart . . ."

"Yes. I know. I'm Sara Jeanne." She pushed open the screen. "Won't you come in?"

It wasn't too wide a door in the first place and with both of us in it, it was a tight enough squeeze that, even scrunched up and going in sideways, I couldn't help brushing up against her a mite — and colored again.

101

"You'll find him in the study — straight ahead," she said. "And now if you'll excuse me I'd better see to my cooking."

Not being the kind what gets easily flubbered I hung fire just long enough to sleeve off the sweat before moving to beard the lion in his den.

With that come-join-me smile, he looked more a daddy of lambs as he poked out a chair for me to sink into and pushed in my direction a box of ten cent stogies.

We lit up and he set back, considering my look through the smoke floating round us. He sighed, shook his head, slanted his eyes at me some more. "What you said about that Sanchez kid hit me a pretty good lick," he growled. "Course I've known right along Hank wasn't no angel, but I hadn't supposed he'd step clean out of line. Findin' her father like that . . . I don't know. It looks bad."

I didn't say anything.

He scrunched up his mouth, took another puff and grimaced. "I'm in kind of a delicate place in this country. Outsider, you know, rep for big interests — buying up land. This could get pretty sticky if that kind of thing was to go on behind my back."

Even I could see he had the right track there. "Trouble is," he said, peering, "the man's not easy to replace," and rolled the smoke across his frown. "Particularly just now. Don't suppose *you'd* feel like working for me would you?"

It was how I'd figured to set up in the first place, but Cap had said no. Still, I got to admit I was mightily tempted, the more so with thoughts of that girl in my head. Looked like he'd been misjudged all around — any guy that was father to a frail like her had to have considerable good in him someplace. Though it did come over me Cap might not think so.

With Mossman in mind I said, sort of dubious; " 'Fraid my feelin's don't come into it. Tell you the truth, I'm tied up now."

His eyes rolled over me. "The Bandle girl?" And, when I nodded, he said without rancor, "Someone mentioned you was out there. But I'm not talking about doctorin' calves. You wouldn't sign on with me for peanuts. There's a future with this company for the right kind of man."

Not pushing, just laying it out for me.

"Anyway," he said, "it's something for you to think about. Of course," he grinned, "you'd have to take care of Ponchatraine."

I could feel my neck heat, but before I could make up my mind if he was daring me, the girl looked in to say grub was on the table. He got up and I trailed after him.

I've no idea what it was I put inside me. Can't honestly remember what we talked about, even. I must've sat plumb lost with the sound of her voice. First thing I caught was him saying with a kind of indulgence: "I'm afraid my niece is inclined to oversimplify. There's been trouble, sure, but it's more what I stand for than myself that these fools are riled at. They don't understand progress."

I opened my mouth and, for a wonder, thought better of it. I don't guess he ever noticed.

"It's always been that way," he went on, warming up to it. "Little minds resent and fear things they don't understand — take what I'm doing as a personal affront."

"An' how would you take it was you in their boots?"

He smiled wryly. "I'm not."

I got up.

He pushed back, too. "Man has to look after himself in this world. If he starts feeling sorry for every Tom, Dick, and Harry . . . Well, I'll keep the offer open. Till I decide, anyway, what to do about Hank."

CHAPTER 12

She was the kind, I imagined, a man would like around the house, someone to come home to. The kind you figured your mother would have been — not the rowdy tomboy sort that would put on pants like some I could name and figure to outdo a man at his own kind of work.

She followed me to the door and when I turned to leave said with a hesitant shyness, "Will you . . . be going to the schoolhouse dance?"

When I stared she colored, pretty as a little pink wagon.

"Didn't even know there was going to be one."

She nodded, nervous. "Sunday a week," she said, dropping her eyes to run the side of one shoe, kind of aimless like, along a crack between boards. "I don't suppose, working for Straddlebug and all, you would find it convenient to . . . well, to carry me, would you?" and jerked up her eyes like a startled doe, all pink and white and so confused I said before half thinking: "Ma'am, I'd be plumb *proud* to fetch you!"

You'll reckon Pearly Adams for the world's biggest chump. Dollars to doughnuts this was Lockhart's conclusion when he learned what a yank I had give to the bait. But it was pretty near worth it — getting bathed in the look them green eyes give me, till I remembered what was tied to the back of my saddle. Them mail order duds sure hadn't been sent for to put on no cows!

I found plenty of time on the way back to Dowling's to look the thought over. Nor was that all I had to gnaw at me. The more I remembered the less comfortable I got. Whatever hid cards was tucked into this deal one thing stood out about as plain as plowed ground: Dallas Lockhart to Belle Bandle was the devil with both his horns on. And what she'd think about me carrying his niece . . .

Lordy, lordy! It was enough to set fire to a white oak post.

I could see a kind of self-pitying fashion how right Cap had been nursing doubts about me. Man might as well face it. Some galoots never found enough sense to pound sand down a gopher hole, and it sure was beginning mighty powerful to look like you-know-who could be one of 'em.

Time I come into the Walking M yard, I had worked me through some considerable thinking without finding anything changed for the better. There seemed a pretty fair chance from what I'd seen of that Curly pelican this outfit and me was rushing headlong to a parting of the ways.

I wasn't going to shed no tears about that — not with Sara Jeanne to think back on; but what about Fletch? He was the only loose end I'd found to get my teeth into.

Not that I'd got so gosh-awful far! I hadn't found one dang bootprint to moon at. There'd been tracks to spare. Half the horses in the Great Staked Plains, it looked like, had been through that yard one time or another. They was no help at all. But to my way of thinking this spread was the nub of it; it was here he'd disappeared from. And whatever was brewing was like to break here again.

More than anything else it was because of this conviction I had passed up Lockhart's offer. And, regardless of what a whole heap of folks figures, the griefs of this life just don't turn away because a guy, like a ostrich, refuses to look at them. I knew I'd piled up a big wheel of trouble and there was no use waiting for Wishbone's lip to catch up with me.

I left my horse by the steps and, squaring my shoulders, pounded Belle's door.

Set me back a bit to have Curly open it. "You fetch that package?" she called over his shoulder.

"Sure," I said, thrusting it at him. "Glad to find you here — saves repeatin' myself. Big thing is I done my eatin' at Lockhart's."

I was braced for an explosion, but if Curly was surprised he done a good job of hiding it. Nothing more to be read from his mug than from a rock.

Standing there aside of him Belle Bandle said, "We're listening."

"Yeah," I said. "Well, first thing that happened I had a run-in with Ponchatraine, Lockhart's mover. He seen it, practically offered me Hank's job."

No fireworks come out of that one, either. Belle just stood there, eyes prowling my face, never showing no more what she thought than him.

"So," Curly said with the beginnings of a grin, "not blind to the benefits, you naturally took it." And, slapping his thigh, he burst into a guffaw.

I stared from one to the other of them, managing finally to haul up my jaw. "What kinda varmint do you reckon you hired?"

Belle Bandle cried: "You passed it up!" like she thought I ought to been bored for the simples.

Disgust was livid on Curly's face. The girl said, "Why, you little lost lamb, we could've clobbered him proper!"

She looked sure enough at the end of her limb.

"Never mind," Curly growled and, at me: "Let's have the rest of it. You tied on the nosebag."

I still didn't get it.

"That's about the size of it." I chucked them back a few looks of my own, him and her both, wondering where I had missed the boat. You'd think, by grab, they had *wanted* me to rat on them!

Belle said, "I expect you just sat there like bumps on a log."

"He's got a niece livin' with him. She done most of the talking."

"You tellin' us he never tried to change your mind?"

"Oh, he tried," I said. "Told me what a future there was for the right kind of man — didn't push it none, though. I don't reckon he's so big for greed as some folks around have made him out. It's just he's got this job —"

"Yeah. Too bad about him. Don't suppose he said what he's done with Fletch Dowlin'."

I had no answer for that. "It didn't come up. He knew I'd been doctorin' cows for you though."

"I'll bet," Curly said. "He probably knows what the cook's got fer supper."

In the midst of our staring, things began to seep through to me. Him coming out of this house last night. Her sending me off to pick up them dresses and him letting it stand while half his crew practically slept in the saddle watching them cows.

That was what he'd been doing here, hatching it up, guessing I'd run into that sonofabitch Hank and figuring, if I didn't get planted, Lockhart would probably do just what he had done, offer to put me in Ponchatraine's boots.

Only, somewhere along, they had figured I'd take it, after which they would fix it to get them a spy. I wondered what inducement they had figured would make me do it.

"He could still change his mind," Belle said, looking hopeful.

"I dunno," Curly growled. "That guy's no chump. Any jigger that could git rid of Fletch an' all his hands — not t' mention them cattle — slick as he done ain't going to —" He spat. "Hell, you better think up something else."

"Hire some more hands."

He said, looking at me, "I can't half watch what we got right now! Anyway it's the wrong time of year. To lick this thing we got to all pull together."

"You want I should call another meeting?"

With his stare still rummaging me, Curly, doubling his fists, disgustedly swore. But I had already heard that E-string bellow that passed for singing with Curly's birddog and, attracted now by the plopping of hoofs, turned to find the old man with a knee round the horn jogging up the lane from the Charleston road.

Curly sent him a shout and Wishbone interrupted his progress toward the corrals to cut over. Pulling up by the porch he swayed, peering owlishly, not quite drunk enough to fall off his saddle. "Back the shame day," he mumbled, grinning foolish like.

"You didn't tell me, boss, we had a guy in thish outfit could sh-sh-shoot the wings off a bot wi-wi-without half tryin'." He pulled off his disreputable hat, grinning hugely, managing to send me a bow. "I've sheen it all now."

Curly looked half minded to sock him. But Belle, stepping in front of him, said, "Are you talking about *Adams?*"

"Betcher life I am. Best damn shot thish shide of the Pecos!" And he proceeded with gestures to describe how (by luck) I had humbled Hank Ponchatraine in front of half of Charleston.

Belle's eyes glowed. She looked at me fondly. "He can still get the job," she said excitedly.

While Curly stood considering, one eye digging into me, I said straight flat, "He ain't goin' to, though."

Belle's eyes spun back at me. "Why not?" she demanded. Without waiting for an answer she said, "Can't you get it through your head that bunch aims to clobber us? There ain't nothing Lockhart won't do to put this spread among the syndicate brands — hell, his tongue's hangin' out a foot an' forty inches!"

"That's still no proof he had any part in whatever it was took off with Fletch Dowlin'. I don't think —"

"Since when has anybody paid you t' think?" Curly said, swelling up, starting towards me belligerent.

I pushed out a hand. But it wasn't till I'd sent the other one hipward that he changed his mind about taking hold of me.

He didn't look scairt — more riled than anything, settling into his tracks like a sore-footed bear. "Long as you hold down a job with this outfit you'll do what you're told." He looked to see if I'd swallowed it. "Now git back to your calfs."

CHAPTER 13

Getting back to them calfs wouldn't butter no parsnips.

Cap had sent me here to head off trouble and seemed like to me it was time I got at it — but what trouble? Where? Only thing remotely suggestive of trouble, if you discounted the scowls and loud talk flapped around, was this business of Dowling.

Any way you looked it was a mystifying muddle. Not so much his disappearing because, for reasons of his own, he could of plain walked off. But the way of it . . . the completeness of the thing was what kept boogering me. And that book on the chair arm.

One feller taking off a guy could understand. And cattle can be rustled — but the whole crew? All the horse stock, too?

When I was sure they couldn't see me from the yard I considered Snuffy's ears and sent him angling toward that road ranch.

First I'd heard of Fletch Dowling had been there in Bolton's bar. Kind of seemed a good place to start scratching.

Hunting the Walking M hadn't turned up a thing. What looking they'd done hadn't strained no eyes. Curly and that girl had been a heap more interested in making doubly sure the spread stayed out of Lockhart's hands. But Lockhart, far as I could see, had made no move to grab it. There had been no harassment of any sort.

Time we reached the river the sun was heeled far over. The claybank was beginning to exhibit signs of wear and tear. I was tired myself. Likewise I was wondering, short of telling the truth, how I was going to explain not getting back for supper. But having come this far I reckoned I might as well push on. I was wrapped in this thinking when the reaching crash of a shot snapped Snuffy back on his haunches and me doubled forward against the horn.

I hadn't been struck but I let myself go, tumbling off the far side to sprawl into a roll that carried me breathless to the base of some brush. Snuffy stood fast. The echoes of that rifle went slapping and fading off into the hills, finally petering out.

I lay facing upslope, eyes grimly quartering the trapped heat and blue shadows.

Whoever had fired was somewhere in them trees higher up. I focused on the most likely site, the fan-shaped root system of a fallen pine. It was too far away to be reached with a pistol; knowing this I edged away from the brush, got one knee under me and, with nothing better in sight, made a run for that mass of torn-up roots.

Reached them. But there was nobody there.

He had been, though. I could see the marked ground where he'd crouched, an empty cartridge case. With a lot of wild thoughts pounding through my head I took a hard look around, found more tracks and, gun up, followed them.

They fetched me to the crest of the rise. I found where his horse had stood, but beyond the fact someone didn't much like me I was no wiser now that I'd been the first place. The ambusher had pulled up stakes and gone. I couldn't even be sure what direction he'd taken. The tracks petered out on a stretch of hard ground, heading, when I lost them, arrow-straight for Dowling's ranch.

Which likely didn't mean a thing. At least I knew damn well if I had been in his boots I'd of done considerable circling before I struck out for home.

Sure I thought about Curly. Ponchatraine, too. And that guy who'd suggested I ask Dowling for a job. But when I got back to Snuffy I still wasn't sure if somebody'd tried to rub me out or just set me up for a scare.

The shadows were beginning to thicken now considerable. In another half hour it was going to be dark.

I rode down to the road ranch, still thinking about it. There was nothing to look at around the yard. Leaving my horse at the porch, I tramped inside making plenty of noise. The bar was empty.

Bolton stepped in from the back, the look of inquiry falling off his chops to be replaced with a scowl when his glance picked me out.

"Hi," I said.

"We're not open fer business."

"Since when?"

His scowl deepened. He said belligerently, "Since ten o'clock this mornin'. I'm fixin' to sell out."

"Well, lucky you." I grinned, and hung a foot on the rail. *Be a hard nut to crack,* I thought. "Alls I want right now," I told him, "is a meal."

His look turned stubborn. It was plain he was fixing to turn me down when his glance, falling away, brushed my hip and bounced off. I translated this to mean the word had

117

got around.

"Well," he grumbled, "if you don't mind takin' it from the wife an' kids . . ." Hating me, he bitterly wheeled and slap-slapped his guarachas back through the curtain.

I listened to the angry mutter of voice sounds, the bang of a skillet against stove metal and thought to myself them kids was powerful quiet.

Fingering the circled star in my pocket I tried to think what I ought to do next. Now that I was here, the trip seemed a fool's errand. If the cattle had passed through Bolton's hands I wasn't likely at this late date to find proof of it.

"A Ranger is resourceful," I remembered Cap saying and on the chance of maybe getting a lead from Bolton's wife, I pushed through the curtain and on across a room with nothing but a bed in it to pause before a door that obviously led to the kitchen. It was not quite shut and as I reached for the knob a man's voice — not Bolton's — said, "He ain't goin' to like this."

I yanked open the door.

Bolton's jaw dropped where he stood above the skillet and across the room a long-haired galoot, half-turned, stood frozen in shock. It was the skinny jasper that had tossed Dowling's name at me the first time

I'd been here. Right hand blurring he spat out a curse. Flame lanced from his hip as I flung myself sideways, that slug whacking into the door.

Things got kind of foggy. I remember coming up off the floor, lungs full of gun stink, clawing for my shooter. Along in there someplace Bolton, trying to get past, clobbered me with the skillet. With my eyes full of roman candles I heard glass crash, the pound of boots. When I begun to take notice and the room quit spinning I found myself peering up at a busted window.

Time I reached it there was nothing to shoot at, nothing at all in that gloom shrouded yard but the diminishing rumor of hard running horses.

I went through the place, taking long enough to make a thorough job of it, even poking around through them sheds and shacks, not forgetting the corrals. There was no woman around, no evidence there had been, no kids of course and no sign of Bolton or his gun-throwing friend.

I poured myself a stiff slug at the bar, found some oats for Snuffy and, when I couldn't postpone the inevitable no longer, climbed into my hull and struck out for headquarters.

A feller needed more light than I had if he

figured to do a halfway job of tracking. Curly would be just as hot as I was to get to the bottom of this, I believed, and he certain sure had the right to be in on it. Might be he'd know who that long-hair was.

It was after ten and the ranch was dark when I pulled into the yard, still beating my head against the why of that business. *He ain't goin' to like it,* that gunslick had cried, but that didn't make no sense to me either. Were they talking about that potbellied loafer, the guy who had been in the bar with him that first time? Didn't seem unlikely — but what wouldn't he like? Bolton feeding me?

Nothing about this deal had made sense from the time I'd first lamped that Walking M sign. It had been dark here then and I was still in the dark, and with that grumbling thought I crawled into my bunk.

When I come up to the cook shack the following morning Curly was standing there waiting by the door.

CHAPTER 14

It was plain before he opened his mouth he wasn't just standing there to prop up no building. His eyes was like two coals in a bucket. "Hold up a minute, Adams." They had the same glittery look I'd seen the morning he'd wanted to string me up.

He waved the rest of them on.

"Now then," he said, "we was one plate short at grubpile last night."

There didn't seem any use beating around through the bushes. "I got to thinking about Dowlin' and went over to Bolton's."

I looked for a sign but if there was one I missed it. So I gave him the run-down, holding nothing back.

He heard me out. "Let's git this straight. You some kind of dick?"

I peered at him, jolted. "You don't give a damn what happened to Dowlin'?"

"Not unless you can pin it on Lockhart."

"But the guy —"

"I'm not his keeper! Hell's fire," Curly snarled, "I got enough on my hands tryin' to run two spreads with a one-spread outfit, not t' mention keepin' this one out of Lockhart's grab! If the guy ain't dead, he's dug for the tules — bought off or scairt off. Any nump could see that!"

Except it didn't go far enough. There was too many things that didn't gee around here. I grumbled, "What was that pair cookin' up over the skillet? Why'd that longhair go for his hardware an' then take off? Bolton, too! An' where was the woman — an' them kids Bolton mentioned?"

"Far's I know Bolton never had a woman." He peered at me, testily.

"Somethin' dang peculiar about that outfit. If I was ranchin' that close seems to me I'd look into it. For all we know that's where Dowlin's cattle went, an' *yours* could be next." I glared, warming up to it. "An' that skinny galoot — where does he fit into this?"

"I never seen no such critter. Probably one of Ponchatraine's range roughers if you didn't just dream him up." He stood undecided, like he was turning something over. Looked at me harder. "It's a cinch," he said, "you won't rest till you know, so go ahead an' look. Poke around if you want to. If Bolton's had an offer, Lockhart's got t' be back of it. Maybe you can turn somethin' up we could use to git that sonofabitch off our backs."

He rasped a hand across the scratch of his jowls. "But you be back here tonight. Miz Belle's callin' a meeting. Some of them greasy-sackers Ponchatraine's gunnies ain't managed to move yet."

I dawdled at the table till the rest of them pulled out. Then I got out the makings and rolled up a smoke. "That feller that tends bar at that road ranch over against the river," I said. "Know anything about him?"

"Only what's common knowledge."

"Such as?"

"Well," Coosie said, "when you come right down to it, nothin' at all."

"Do you know if he's married?"

The cook shook his head. "Why all the interest?"

I told him about last night. His eyes got big when I mentioned the gunplay. But he didn't offer any comment. I described Bolton's skinny companion.

"Don't fit nobody I ever got a look at."

"Think he's one of Hank's outfit? Spyin' on us, maybe?"

Coosie dumped his pots in the tub.

123

"Plenty of guys on the dodge driftin' through these hills." Then he said, half turning to look over his shoulder, "Could be just another ranny huntin' a place to hole up. Could of figured you was showin' a mite too much interest, goin' back like you done."

I tried another thought. "How long's Curly been ramroddin' Straddlebug?"

Coosie's stare turned blank and his face along with it. "Button," he said, "you better git the hell outa here!"

The road ranch, when I got back to it that morning, looked about like it had the first time I saw it. Only this time, plainly there was nobody home. No sign of life about the place at all.

I went through it again. No evidence of anyone having been held or buried for that matter. If Dowling was dead there was nothing to suggest he'd been killed on the premises.

I found the tracks of the horses that pair had got away on, found where they'd split up a couple miles farther on. Nothing to show which was which so I stayed with the tracks that swung into the higher hills.

As the going got rougher the sign became a heap harder to read. He'd done considerable anti-godlin around and was walking his horse when the tracks petered out on a stretch of loose shale.

Beyond that was a ledge sloping down toward the river. I cut a few circles without picking him up again. It was plain as the horn on a saddle he had someway got himself into that water but I couldn't find where, nor where he'd come out. Seemed a pretty good chance he'd kept to that river right on into town.

I done the same.

If he'd gone into town he'd probably hit a bar and by this time I was in the mood to hoist a few myself. I come out below the bridge and went into the first dive I come to. No sign of Bolton or the other one either, but I had me a beer. The place was practically empty, just the barkeep down at the far end catching up with events as recorded in week-old copy of the *Tombstone Epitaph.* About midway down, between him and me, a pair of townies in button shoes was discussing some dame they called Flossie.

I finished my beer and turned into another place two doors up.

It was enjoying a somewhat livelier trade, but among the faces there was none I knew. Back on the street I stood looking around.

By the hang of my shadow it was considerable past noon and I reckoned if I was going to be back for that meeting I was pretty soon going to have to raffle my hocks.

Seemed like all I'd been doing so far was mark time. Aside from the mystery of Dowling's disappearance I hadn't seen anything that called for a Ranger, nor heard anything to warrant Cap's hunch. Still, there was that business last night to confound my notion this might all be a mare's nest. If there was nothing to hide, why had Bolton and that other bird taken off like they had? There had to be reason back of that gunplay.

The two likeliest places where the temper and thinking of a community could be measured, speaking generally of course, would be its bars or a general store. In this town the store was owned by a syndicate Lockhart represented; to loiter there would invite suspicion. With this thought in mind I tried another dive, a honkytonk this time with girls, the whole works.

It was a big oblong room with doors off a balcony for private entertainment. Most of the gambling rigs were still covered but even at this hour some play was in progress. One faro layout was taking bets, and off in a corner five gents sat at poker with ten or twelve more bellied up to the bar. And one of them was Bolton.

He stood off by himself scowling into his glass.

I felt more foolish than anything. Now that I'd found him, what the hell could I do? I could brace him, sure. I had questions, enough, but no way at all to make him part with any facts. He had as much right to be here as I had.

If it had been that skinny longhair now. . . .

Matching his scowl I stood fidgeting, uncertain. Snorting with disgust, I retreated to the street and, filled with frustration, stepped around the hitchrail thinking I might as well pull out. I could whip the socks off that whoppy-jawed bucko, but couldn't put no faith in any answers that might fetch me.

I'd come into this country bound to make Cap proud of me, and what had I accomplished? Not a goddam thing! I might's well be pounding my head against a bucket. I had tried to hang and rattle, figuring on a break, but I just couldn't get my teeth into nothing. It was like punching cobwebs.

Still fuming, fed up with it, I was looking around for a dog to kick when Lockhart's niece, arms crammed with bundles, come out of the company store. She seen me, too.

And across the width of the road she smiled.

Yanking loose Snuffy's reins, I was fixing to join her when the dive's louvered doors, pushed half open by an outcoming body, caught my notice by stopping in mid swing. Across their tops two startled eyes in a drop-jawed face locked with my own in panicked consternation.

The face jerked back. The door slapped shut.

Though froze in my tracks, recognition was mutual. I wasn't about to forget that pelican or the slug he'd thrown at me in Bolton's kitchen — *this longhaired bastard who'd advised me to hit Fletch Dowling for a job!*

Roaring out of my trance I went under the rail and through them doors like a bat out of Carlsbad.

I couldn't see too good with the change in light but there wasn't nothing hazy about the way my arms clamped onto that reeling body, barreling him back until he smashed against the bar.

Pinning him there with the wealth of my fury I slammed a pile driving right hard against his jaw — and another! Then I stepped back and watched him slide to the floor.

Sure I felt good. I felt seven foot tall standing over that whippoorwill. Now, by God, I'd find out a few things!

The awful quiet in that place was just beginning to catch up with me when the doors slapped again and a rough voice growled: "What the hell you think you're doin' there, feller?"

He spun me around, shoved a gun in my ribs.

I was riled all over but not too graveled to see the badge on his shirt or the flaming red hair above those hardbitten brawler's features.

This was the Bogy Red I'd heard about, described a hundred times as Judge Burnett's hard-drinking town marshal.

I said, "This sonofabitch tried to kill me last night."

He peered at me like I'd two heads or something. "You don't have to take my word for it," I told him. "Ask Bolton over there —"

But when I twisted to point him out to the marshal, Bolton, of course, wasn't there any more. Way the rest of them looked you'd of thought sure as hell I'd raped the town belle or —

"Somebody git the doc over here. Mister," Red said, "you're comin' with me!"

I tried to think of some way I could make

him believe me, but what way was there now that Bolton had bolted? I growled, "At least lock him up — make sure he doesn't get away. Get Lockhart over here. He'll vouch . . ."

Something staring back at me out of Red's face twitched me round to look again. It was just like someone put a foot in my guts. That guy on the floor *was* Lockhart.

CHAPTER 15

I must of flapped my gills like a fish out of water. It *couldn't* be Lockhart, but by God it was! Right there where I'd knocked him. Draped over that rail like a gutted slut.

Lordy, lordy!

A muscle twitched in his cheek; a kind of groan shuddered out of him. Bogy Red wasn't fixing to wait. He nudged me again with the snout of that hogleg, perking his chin in the direction of the doors. "Movin' time, mister. Walk or git carried."

I suppose I walked. I don't remember being carried. With my skull like a stamp mill pounding out notions, each wilder than the next, only thing I got any sure recollection of was the astonished dismay on the face of Sara Jeanne as we went past her buggy. My thoughts right then was ten for a penny.

Remember me telling you about Charleston's jail — that deep pit in the ground with the stake in the center to which prisoners were chained? Well, that was where I wound up, shackled and padlocked like a hydrophoby killer.

All the time he was getting me in there, I was considerable exercised over Bogy Red finding that badge in my pocket. But I needn't have worried. He never bothered to search me, just took away my pistol.

It wasn't till the two guards climbed out with the key to that padlock that the full force of my predicament hit me. Considering Lockhart's standing, his influence in this country, it come over me my prospects was a long ways from salubrious.

I watched Bogy Red help the last guy out. "For cripes sake," I yelled. "Don't I even get a hearin'?"

"You'll git heard when the judge gits around to it."

"What about grub?"

"What about it?" he said, and with that went off and left me.

I had plenty of thoughts to pass the time with, none of them happy and some downright wretched. Like the probable notions of Curly and Belle when I didn't turn up for that meeting tonight. Like Sara Jeanne's feelings when she found out what I had done to her uncle. I didn't touch on *his* thoughts; I had troubles enough without borrowing from that quarter. I worked up most of my sweat trying to figure out how and precisely what happened.

Lockhart, I decided, must have been approaching them doors, bound for the street, when Long Hair — spotting me — ducked back around him. Nothing else appeared to make any sense. Long Hair, of course, must have left by the back, or gone out through a window like he'd done last night. But where had that son of a buck *come* from?

For the matter of that where had Lockhart? I'd looked over that joint, hadn't seen either one of them — nobody but Bolton at the bar's far end standing there scowling into the bottom of his glass.

Then it come to me. Of course! They'd been up on the balcony behind them closed doors!

I prodded that around more than a little before accepting it. I reckoned they could, mighty easy, have been up there with doves — that was what I wanted to think, neither of them knowing the other was anywhere around. But I couldn't quite stretch credulity that far. No one but a halfwit would believe this wasn't a rendezvous.

He won't like it. I could still hear Long Hair saying that to Bolton just before I'd stepped in to kick the lid off. Was the *he* referred to

Lockhart? Was this skinny pistolero one of Two-Pole Pumpkin's understrappers? the source of Lockhart's knowledge of affairs at Walking M? That longhaired whippoorwill had come in to report, to maybe tell about my snooping, get his orders what to do.

I sure didn't want to believe it, but couldn't see no other answer.

Lockhart had a job to do. And, no matter how you sliced it, he had not been above hiring Ponchatraine to help.

Some ways right then it began to seem like to me I'd cut my string considerable short when I'd turned down Lockhart's offer. Looked like Curly and Belle was nearer right than I had thought for.

With Sara Jeanne tugging hard I tried to believe her uncle and this skinny jigger had been in that dive unbeknownst to each other, but it was just too much for a feller to swallow, him coming through them doors like he had split seconds after Long Hair had been taking his peek at me.

I don't know when I first noticed it, but quite a crowd had presently collected to peer down into that hole at me. They weren't saying much, and nothing to me, but several of them weren't above grinning encouragement at the brash damn fool who had done what probably a lot of them had wanted to. I wasn't much set up by this, knowing any darn chump who'll take a poke at authority can always find others willing to egg him on.

Bogy Red come around after a while and run them off.

Soon as I was sure I wasn't being observed I dropped that circled star into my boot — and none too soon. For scarcely had I straightened than Red was back with his pair of helpers. With the chain unshackled I was hauled up out of there, hungry enough to eat a hide with the hair on.

Turned out they hadn't come to feed me, though nobody bothered to put me wise. I hadn't no suspicion of what was coming off till they hustled me through that honky-tonk's batwings and shoved me, grumbling, up in front of an old geezer in a stovepipe hat. Red, stiffening then like a guy getting ready to salute the flag, sent a hard look around and cried like a tent show barker: "Hear ye, hear ye! This Court'll come to order!" And he banged on the bar with his sixshooter till all roundabout talk had been hammered into silence. "His Honor, Judge Burnett, presidin'!"

"What case is this?" the old geezer asked.

Bogy said, "Two-Pole Pumpkin versus Adams."

"And the charge?"

"Felonious assault. With battery. Company charges this defendant, Pearly Adams — drifter — did willfully and with malice attack and clobber its legal representative, one Dallas Lockhart, resident manager, on these here premises at two thirty-eight of this same afternoon."

A breathy quiet had fallen over the place rasped by the rustle of necks being craned. The old fart stared like I was some kind of bug. "How do you plead?" he says, sticking his lip out.

I was fed to the neck with being pushed around or I might have trimmed my words more careful — which is not to say I wouldn't of popped off, riled and resentful as I was right then. What I said was, loud and indignant: "What kinda deal am I getting here anyway? Where's the jury — ?" I had more on my mind, but that was as far as I was able to get through the clatter and smash of Red's hammering gun butt.

When a modicum of quiet had been restored, Burnett rolled his eyes at me and said: "This Court is old enough to make up its own mind," and cocked his head to the chorus of titters.

Bogy Red pounded the bar again. Burnett rasped: "We'll have respect in this room or the bailiff with clear it." He looked around grim like, hunched his shoulders, said, "Where's defendant's counsel?"

"Your Honor," Red grumbled, "he never asked fer none."

Burnett's stare took hold of me again. "Are you prepared to conduct your own defense, Adams?"

"I don't recognize your right to try me," I said. "You been off the bench —"

"That'll do!" he snapped, wattles red and shaking. "For your information," Bogy Red piped up, "His Honor's been reappointed. Now answer the question."

"I don't *know* any shysters."

Burnett said, "This Court will appoint —"

"Don't bother," I growled, and saw his mouth snap shut.

"Very well. How do you plead?"

"Well . . . hell. I didn't set out to —"

"This Court is not interested in what defendant *didn't* do. It seeks only to find whether you struck Mister Lockhart."

"Then," I said, resigned to it, "I'll have to plead guilty. But, the way it happened —"

"Defendant's side will be heard at the proper time. Where is the complainant?"

"Your Honor," said somebody getting up behind me, "complainant is in no condition to be here account of defendant attacking and brutally beatin' him within a inch of his life."

"That's a goddam lie!" I yelled, jumping up. And, ignoring the racket of Bogy Red's gun butt, I twisted around to get a look at the varmint, not too astonished to find I had once again to deal with Hank Ponchatraine. I was surprised though at the way he backed off from me, acting like he feared I was about to bust his face in.

Bogy Red grabbed hold of me. Ponchatraine with his eyes bugged out threw up one arm as though to ward me off. "Hang onto that crazy fool 'fore he kills me — *he's already* tried twice! Last time with half the town lookin' on!"

Burnett said above the snout of a pistol, "Another outburst like that and I'll clear this room. Bailiff! Fetch Adams over here; and you" — he barked at Lockhart's mover — "stand over by that faro layout and don't open your mouth again till you're spoke to!"

When his orders had been complied with, the Judge, still glowering, laid his hardware handy on the table in front of him and, directing his words again at Hank said, "Let's get into this record your name and place of residence."

"Henry Ponchatraine. Two-Pole Pumpkin."

"Bailiff, administer the oath."

Bogy Red did so.

"Now then," Burnett said, "you're employed by that company?"

Ponchatraine nodded.

"In what capacity?"

"Foreman."

"Are you appearing in that role on behalf of your employer?"

"I am, Your Honor."

"All right. You may stand down for the moment. Now Marshal," Burnett said, turning to Bogy Red again, "kindly tell this Court as briefly as possible what you found when sounds of a disturbance brought you on a run to these premises at" — he consulted some notes beside his pistol — "at two thirty-eight of this p.m."

Red, with an appreciative look around at his audience, cleared his throat with considerable authority. "Well, Your Honor, at the time hostilities must of broken out I —"

Burnett said impatiently, "Just tell us what you found."

Bogy said with his jaw stuck out, "I found this here defendant standin' over Lockhart which was on the floor against the foot of the bar there, blood all over an' stone cold out. This feller" — jabbing a finger at me — "had a look in his eyes —"

"What's he tryin' to do to me?" I cried. "I didn't slaughter the guy! I only hit him twice. And remarks about how I looked calls for a conclusion —"

"I don't know what you're getting at, Adams. The man's within his rights. An expert in violence with a world of experience. As town marshal, and a deputy under Sheriff Johnny Behan —"

"That don't prove he can't make a mistake! I was mixed up myself. I'd just come out of this place, fixin' to get on my horse. Some guy took a shot at me last night — I'd just trailed him here from Bolton's road ranch. I didn't see him inside but as I reached for my reins them doors streaked open. It was the guy I'd been hunting. He ducked back. I piled through them doors, got hold of somebody which I figured was him. It was hard to see after that glare outside. When he tried to get away I popped him. Twice. Next thing I know I'm under arrest —"

"I got witnesses," Red busted in belligerently. "Nobody has to take my word for anything. They seen the same thing I did."

"Are your witnesses present?" the Judge said grumpily.

Bogy Red called them out of the crowd. Six there was, as rough looking a lot as you would hope to run into. Ponchatraine give me a nasty grin.

"Well," Burnett said, "what did you see?"

They peered at each other, then one of them said, "We seen this Adams come tearin' through them batwings, latch onto Lockhart, slam him reelin' into the bar. Then he jumps him again, starts workin' him over. When the pore devil couldn't take any more an' falls helpless on the floor, this guy starts t' put the boots to him. Woulda killed him sure as I'm a foot high if the Marshal here hadn't drug him off — never seen a guy so fired up t' do murder."

And the other five nodded.

Burnett said to me sternly: "You want to sound off again before I pass sentence?"

"Damn right!" I snarled, so mad I was shaking. "There wasn't six horses tied outside. Look at them fellers — you ever see 'em before? Ask if they're employed an', if they are, what spread they work for. An' make sure this time they're swore in to tell the truth —"

"That won't be necessary," drawled a voice from somewhere in the direction of the doors.

Heads twisted. Eyes bugged out, my own included, to find Lockhart standing there, cool as you please.

CHAPTER 16

Nobody figured to be more astonished than Hank Ponchatraine, though Burnett, I give in, looked to run him a close second. Popped up like a Jack-in-the-Pulpit, cheeks rapidly darkening with outrage, he stood gripping the table like he couldn't believe it.

"Oh, it's me, right enough," Lockhart said smiling thinly. "I've no quarrel with Adams. This farce was rigged without my knowledge — they've been using you, Judge, to pay off a grudge."

His glance, cold as froglegs, cut past the six to settle on Hank like a forefooting rope. "Ponchatraine," he said without lifting his voice, "you've had your last meal on Two-Pole Pumpkin. As of right now you're through, done, finished. Pick up your time at my office and, when you pull out, take those six liars with you."

The stillness was thick enough to chop

with an axe.

Then Burnett, quavery with fury, cried: "Marshal! Arrest —"

"No you don't!" Hank growled, backing off, sixgun weaving; and the other six lost no time following suit. Nobody else when Red stood rooted showed any call to get in their way as one by one the six slipped out, dragging their spurs in the direction of the tie rails. Ponchatraine snarled, glowering at Lockhart, "I'll tend to you later!" and, wickedly, whirling, threw down on me.

I let out a yell and dived for the floor, them racketing shots sounding loud as cannons. Three times flame stabbed and only temper and haste kept me from being turned into a colander. First slug missed by as much as a foot; next one grazed my ribs as I rolled, but the third come closer, jerking the wipe where it fluttered at my throat. Then, Burnett, snatching up his shooter, got into it and Ponchatraine, swearing, took after the others, knocking Lockhart sprawling as he banged through the doors.

The place was in an uproar as I clawed to my feet. I done my best to get out on the street but every guy and his uncle, now it was safe, was bound the same place. A rattle of hoofs fell back off the buildings and guys by then was so thick round the doors there couldn't no one get through till it was too late to stop them.

Time I got out there wasn't nothing but dust, and mighty little of that, to show which way that bunch had cleared out by. "To hell with 'em," somebody said and the crowd, rehashing it, began to break up. I felt a hand on my arm.

It was Lockhart had hold of me. "Let's go some place and habla," he said, so with nothing to lose I went along with him, which isn't to say I wasn't doing some wondering.

Though the cards didn't seem to have fallen that way, the possibility was still in my head I had got the right slant on this deal in the first place. I'd noticed all right no one had any words for him. He might be the Big Auger around these parts but nobody was about to come up and hug him.

There was bars all around — more than enough to shake a stick at — but he went past them all and off down a side street scarcely bigger than your navel to whisk me into El Tio's cantina.

It was a cubbyhole dive with no more than two lamps lit to dispel the gloom of encroaching night, as them word wranglers have it. He preempted a table in the joint's dimmest corner and said nothing at all till a scarfaced waiter had taken our orders and gone off to fetch them.

"What's a man say when he finds he's pulled a bloomer?" Lockhart asked, scowling into his hands. "I knew when I hired him that guy would sour fresh cream, but the sort of job I was sent here to do ain't the kind where a feller runs around waving handkerchiefs. I thought I could keep him in line with high wages . . ."

He broke off as the scarface come lugging the glasses. When the man went away he pushed the bottle toward me. "Fill 'em up," he said. "We're going to drink to better times."

I was all for that. He poured us some more. Swishing the amber around in the glass Lockhart said, sourly moody, "As you can probably imagine, the guy in charge is the last one to know when a thing like this begins to snowball against you. But I was more than a little suspicious already when you told me about that girl the other day.

"Trouble was," he growled, jerking his eyes up, "there was nothing but your word for it and by then I could see he'd just about took over."

I stared, astonished. "You was *scairt* of him?"

Lockhart reddened. "I certainly wasn't

overjoyed at the prospect of tangling with him. And," he said dryly, "I'd got Sara Jeanne to think of — that's why I tried to hire you." His eyes sought his hands again. "I was hoping, that way, you'd get rid of him for me."

Which was sure as hell putting it right on the table.

My opinion of Lockhart went up a couple of pegs. Took a pretty big guy to own up to what he had. In his boots I doubted if I could of done it.

I pushed my glass around, scowling. "Well, you're rid of him now."

"I'd like to believe that."

"You think he'll come back? After them lies an' them slugs he flung round?"

Lockhart scowled, too. "You heard what he told me. Three times he's lost face, the last two in public. He's not apt to forget it."

You couldn't doubt he was worried.

Chewing his lip he looked up again to say in a way no man likes to hear, "I wish by Christ you'd take that job, Adams. You can write your own ticket."

I thought uncomfortably of Belle and Curly; there was two more that wished I would take it. And, like he said, there was Sara Jeanne, alone here in town if anything happened to him, an eastern filly, not understanding this country.

I slogged down my drink. I could see Cap's face plain as if he was standing there. *You won't be getting much help from that bunch.* What he really wanted was a target sure-fire enough to draw Hank's lead and give him time to hunt shelter. He couldn't very well have put it any plainer.

Kind of raised my gorge the more I thought about it. I pinned a hard look on him. "How much do you know about what happened to Dowlin'?"

He eyed me, puzzled. "I don't know anything about it. I supposed he'd pulled out. Why" — his stare suddenly widened — "you trying to tell me Dowling's been killed?"

Instead of answering I said grimly, "That one of the outfits you been fixin' to lay hold of?"

All expression disappeared from his face. "We'll talk about that when your name's on the paysheet."

I snorted, disgusted. "Trust," I said, "is a two-way street. You're strong for your wants but mighty slow to reciprocate." I was proud of that word, glad to find a place to use it. I seen his look kind of darken, his stare clouding up again, but whether from anger or shame I couldn't tell.

"You're turning me down?"

I was minded to, anyhow.

Curly's notions on the subject wasn't based on what I might learn in that job, but strictly on the chances it might furnish for wrecking Lockhart, maybe getting him replaced. But I couldn't forget Cap hadn't approved of it; he had thought I'd get more digging round, a free agent.

Maybe Cap was right. I said, "I'll sleep on it, Dallas," and left him sitting there.

Just the same I couldn't get it out of my head. All the way back to the Walking M the prospect of being range boss for a big ranch outfit like Two-Pole Pumpkin kept tangling with every other thought I tackled. Turned me nervous and irritable and at the same time — half the time, anyway — I seemed to be floating ten foot above ground.

I kept reminding myself he hadn't tied any strings to it. It was up to me, and I could name my own terms.

Where else would I ever get such an offer? What other guy my age could boast of the like, or would paw up the daisies for even two seconds trying to make up his mind!

Lockhart figured to put me out on a limb — but there was the beauty of it. Sure it would get Ponchatraine down on me, but

148

wasn't Hank down on me killing mad anyway? Moneywise and future-wise it was bound to beat Rangering fifty-seven ways!

And that was where the rub come. I didn't figure I owed a second thought to Belle or Curly, yet every time I pictured Cap Mossman it made me feel like a goddam snake.

The night was lowering, sultry, cloud covered. Could be working up to a gully washer by the sticky feel of everything I had on me, though it generally took at this end of the cactus seven, eight days of fooling round in this fashion. The crickets were scratching hammer and tongs and off someplace in the higher hills you could hear an occasional coyote yammer.

Lonesome country. Plenty places for a feller to bed down with a rifle or a bunch of plug-uglies to set up an ambush. Farther I got the more nerves I discovered. "Nope," I told Snuffy, "that Ponchatraine sidewinder ain't goin' to rest easy till he's had another try at rubbin' me out. That's one damn thing we can sure depend on."

I kept getting these spells of keeping my eyes peeled but most of the time I thought about being segundo to Lockhart. Job like that could have its drawbacks. No syndicate outfit I ever heard tell of collected any medals for popularity. Most of them was feared, looked upon with suspicion by the cow spreads around them, and that went double for Two-Pole Pumpkin. Just the. . . .

No light showed at the Walking M when I come in sight of it just short of midnight. The meeting was over, no doubt about that. No rigs in the yard and no tied horses. Belle, I reckoned, would be some put out.

I hauled off my saddle, turned Snuffy into the trap and put up the bars without having reached any real decision. I could hear Cap now. *One thing you can say about a Ranger, boy — there ain't no quit in him.* There was that angle, too, but I had knocked around enough in this world to be sure if you didn't stand up for yourself no one else would.

Still fuming and fretting I heaved my saddle on a pole, blanket spread on top of it, hair side out to dry. Swearing, out of sorts, I headed for the bunkhouse.

I was rounding the yardside corner of the barn when a clicked-back hammer stopped me cold in my tracks.

CHAPTER 17

A voice, clipped and harsh, come out of the shadows. "Gay life pall on you?"

I had reckoned he'd be in a sod-pawing mood. Wasn't no point dredging up any backchat; all I'd ever got from him was trouble.

"Draggin' in here like the Prodigal Son! You know what time of the night this is?"

He was so mad his voice pretty near got away from him as he come out of the gloom, fist full of gun, to stare me up and down like you'd thought he was Moses finding them Jews with the Golden Calf. "I oughta work you over!" he said mean as gar soup thickened with tadpoles, face shoved within two inches of my own. Then he backed off a mite. "What's so goddam funny?"

"A body'd think we was married or something."

He lowered his tone if not his temper. "You outa your mind? I told you Belle wanted you at that meetin' —"

"There's things won't be ordered, not even for Miz Belle. Did you know they've put Burnett back on the bench?"

What Curly said about the Judge could of got him sent to Siberia for life. Then he come up for air, peered at me again, suspicious as a guy with one foot in a boghole. "What's this got t' do with your skippin' that meetin'?"

I told him. About tracking that skinny longhaired galoot, about finding Bolton by himself in that honkytonk and going outside and seeing his sidekick framed in them batwings. About charging through and clobbering Lockhart and getting put into that pit by Bogy Red.

I described my encounter with Judge Burnett and told how Lockhart had sacked the whole caboodle and how Hank and his gunsmiths had broke up the shindig. Only thing I didn't go into at all was that cantina confab between Dallas and me.

For a couple of minutes it got quiet enough to hear the crickets. You could see I'd given him something to think about and he wasn't popping off till he had got it digested.

"So Lockhart's fired that son of a bitch." He kept turning it over like a guy hunting bait; you could pretty near hear the wheels going round. "Maybe," he said, and pulled up his jaw. "Guess this cuts you out of any chance fer that job, knockin' Lockhart around like you done. You think he was there t' meet that bugger?"

"I dunno," I said, surprised to find it was the truth. "He's got to been gettin' his dope on us someplace."

"Yeah," Curly growled, and chewed around on it some more. "Seems likely," he muttered. "We can be sure of one thing. If Bolton's sold out, we've got Lockhart fer a neighbor — ain't no one else kin afford t' buy anythin'."

Next morning early, after he'd laid out the work for the rest of them, Curly ordered me and Buck to saddle up and fetch rifles. While we went off to do it he headed for the house.

"What you reckon he's up to?" I asked myself, knowing dang well I'd get nothing out of Buck. Packing rifles didn't look like no overture to peace and good will.

I said to Buck, "You go to that meetin'?"

He scowled at me sourly. "You didn't miss much. Damn greasy sackers! Guy could git just as far digging a hole with a fiddlestring. All paw an' no beller."

He said after a minute, throwing the hull on his mount, "You'd think, seein' what's happened to some of these other spreads — bein' roughed up or forced t' close out fer peanuts, they'd know it's pull together or git caught short one after the other. Alls Curly wanted was t' set up some alarms so's if one of us got jumped the rest could come a-runnin'. Hell!"

"Wouldn't have no part if it, eh?"

"I ain't heard so many excuses since Ed Brill got caught in that old man's closet. Put the guts of that crowd in your eye and you'd never feel it!"

We sat around in the yard for a spell, then Curly come out looking like a cat with a mouthful of tail feathers. "Let's go!" he growled, and we took out after him hellity larrup.

Way he was heading didn't take no dame with a crystal ball to figure out where this expedition was bound for. By all the signs and signalsmokes, that road ranch was due to get a real shaking up.

Thinking of Bolton fetched Lockhart to mind again, and I could still feel surprise at how understanding for so important an hombre he'd been about the way I had knocked him around. Most of the boss men I had encountered would of been some resentful had they been in his boots, yet not one word had he spoke on the subject. Took a pretty big gent to forget how I had used him.

I wasn't no slouch at forgetting things, either, coming off like I had without recovering my pistol. Built a fire in my cheeks every time my thoughts touched it. My stock with Cap Mossman would drop lower than a snake's belly if a thing like that ever managed to catch up with him — a gunless Ranger would give the crooks a real belly laugh. I could still recall the queer look Curly'd give me before digging up the loan of another.

I done a pile of thinking on that ride to Bolton's, none of it comfortable. I could see mighty clear if I kept on at this rate someone had better get me bored for the simples.

Mostly to blow the horses, I guess, Curly presently slowed the pace as we swung down toward the river. Yet I could see by the determined clamp of his face that whatever had brought on this departure from normal was nothing he figured to harbor second thoughts on.

We splashed across and there was no one in sight when we rode into the yard. The corrals was empty. Near as I could tell Bolton hadn't been back since he'd quit the place with that longhaired jigger that had figured to chalk me up for dead.

Pulling up by the sag of that whoppyjawed porch we sat our saddles with the dust swirling round while Curly, looking grim as death with that rifle, slammed his yell against the weather-grayed walls.

"Hello the house!"

All we got back was a clatter of echoes.

I said, uneasy, "What are we doin' here? What did we come for?"

Curly with his stare still quartering the yard growled, "To make damn sure nobody else moves in."

His smoldering eyes took hold of my face. "We're goin' to have us a bonfire, an' you're goin' t' set it."

"Now wait a minute!" I cried, aghast.

The both of them was grinning. Nothing friendly about it.

"Why *me?*" I grumbled.

"Because I say so," Curly's eyes was nasty. "That's an order, kid."

I was graveled plenty, and that 'kid' he'd tacked onto it wasn't calculated to improve my temper. Thoughts were junin' round in my noggin like flies but the snout of that rifle was pointing right at me.

"You can start with them sheds. Yank up some of that creosote!"

I could see by Buck's mug he hoped for an argument. I could see several things but there wasn't much choice if I hoped to stay healthy. No one but a fool would pull against a cocked rifle. But once I got under cover of them sheds . . .

He was way ahead of me. "Buck, git his hardware."

As Buck swung his horse toward me, careful not to break the rifle's advantage, I kneed mine back enough to keep him from reaching.

He broke out a scowl.

"You want me t' knock you off that nag?" Curly's looks said plain he wasn't going to fool around. I remembered that time he had wanted to hang me. "If you're found in the ashes you'll be blamed for it anyway."

But I couldn't see a Ranger setting fire to someone's property, even no place as ratty as this. Yet that bullheaded bastard meant every damned word of it. He didn't care no more about human life than a range cook would worry about 'weevils in his biscuits.

I had just got down to this hard conclusion when somebody someplace tried to stifle a sneeze.

All three of us froze.

Curly first come out of it. Right then, as he twisted round with a curse, you'd of thought all hell was emigrating on cartwheels. That goddam yard was a-shriek with blue whistlers. Curly's horse went onto its hind legs, squealing. Buck with blood pouring out of his mouth pitched slanchways out of his flown-up saddle.

I snatched up the hogleg Curly had loaned me and triggered three times before it got to me there was nothing coming out of the barrel but wishes. After that I grabbed leather and kicked with both heels.

CHAPTER 18

With all that shooting I still can't figure how I ever got out of that yard in one piece. Someone up there must of really took care of me. I can tell you one thing. Old Snuffy when he finally did pull up wasn't shaking no more than I was. It's a wonder I hadn't plumb ruint him.

I had no idea where we was. Looking round didn't help. Through the wriggles of heat I could see the Huachucas away off to the south. Three times as far east more mountains stuck up, lower these, blue with distance, that like enough was probably the Cherry-cows; but roundabout and in between was nothing I recalled having seen before.

Don't think I was complaining. I was powerful glad just to be at all, glad of the quiet neck deep around us and the grunt of breathing that proved we was there. We was almighty lucky and the both of us knew it.

Half of Snuffy's left ear was gone, with the blood crusted round it looking like a burst boil and, when I got strength enough to get down to feel myself over, eight inches of bullet burn across the flat of his rump was a-crawl with flies. I drove them off with my hat and daubed on some of that screwworm purple but what I kept seeing was what had happened to my headgear.

Half an inch lower and I'd still been in that yard!

It was hard to believe I hadn't been scratched. Way them slugs had been snarling round, it didn't seem possible unless strict orders had been laid down about me. I could, reluctantly, buy this because Bolton had told me he was selling the place and Curly had claimed no one but Lockhart had the price to buy anything. And Lockhart, in that cantana confab, had made me seem pretty essential to his plans.

Still I couldn't help wondering who'd been rodding this bunch. That wasn't no hit-or-miss trap we'd climbed into. Been laid with care and considerable forethought. I could hardly doubt now he had been in that honkytonk to meet Bolton's sidekick. Perhaps to turn over the agreed upon price — for that road ranch, I mean.

Yet in spite of my shudders I was minded

to slip back.

Cap had sent me into this San Pedro country hoping to head off trouble. I don't know what he thought I could do. There hadn't seemed to be any very sharp indications unless you believed Dallas Lockhart's backers were out to gobble this whole jag of range.

I had been some reluctant to take that view. It seemed too obvious, too preposterous after talking to the man, though I won't say Sara Jeanne mightn't of tipped the scales a little. But every jigger I'd bumped into seemed a sight too inclined to take it for granted everything they didn't like Dallas Lockhart was back of.

Buying up range — even leaning on folks a little, was commonplace methods in the West of this time; but driving out people that didn't want to sell was going too far I thought, and it was told pretty plain that Two-Pole Pumpkin wasn't drawing no lines even at downright murder.

But where was the evidence? Talk is never cheaper than the kind you get from belly-achers. It's the have-nots always make the most noise.

And the dispossessed weren't no longer around. Nor was Fletch Dowling — least-ways not around to know about. Not around to get hold of, certainly.

I brought to mind that Mex girl, Connie. Her, anyways, I had seen myself, having watched Hank Ponchatraine push her around. But she was gone, too, and her old man dug from an abandoned shaft. You might suspect foul play but who would you pin it on? Ponchatraine?

Lockhart, to me, had frankly admitted the syndicate range boss might be taking on himself decisions he hadn't any authority to make. Probably had a tough crew. I could go along with that, even conceded that on occasion they might tend to get out of hand. Yet with so much smoke there was bound to be some fire. Which didn't have to mean Dallas Lockhart was privy to it.

Such was the way this had shaped up till now: It hadn't been Lockhart who'd proposed burning Bolton's. But, much as she hated everything Dallas stood for, it hadn't been Belle that had set up the trap we had just ridden into. And it damn sure wasn't Curly.

Seemed like if I was ever to get my teeth into anything, the place to do it was that tumbledown road ranch, and before those ambushers pulled their freight. With Buck and Curly pretty sure to be dead, they was bound to see, if I could make it to Belle's, we would turn every man out. They would hardly expect me to come back alone.

This was how I sized it up anyways.

But it was plain I'd never reach Walking M quick enough for us to catch them jokers redhanded — I didn't know where the spread was from here. Or Charleston, either. I'd left tracks coming from Bolton's, could likely make out to follow them back. Unless I did and could get close enough to catch a look at them sidewinders there'd be no chance of pinning this onto anyone. I knew the risk all right, but that was the clincher.

A glance at my shadow showed I'd been away the best part of an hour. I was still plenty jumpy but I was riled now too, resentful enough to want to do something about it.

My horse was in no shape to run races but I pushed him along as fast as I dared. It was still crowding ten, with the sun getting fiercer every step we took, time I found myself looking down at the river and that collection of relics Bolton called a ranch.

The place looked abandoned, no horses in sight and no detectable movement — but the sweat come out on me just peering at it. It had looked plumb harmless and empty before.

Which was when I remembered to dig out

that pistol.

Five out of six of the shots was loaded, the brass winking up with a Judas smile. Every shell had its bullet. I shook them into my hand. Wasn't a pin mark on one of them — goddam hammer was filed smooth as a pool ball!

And this was the gun Curly'd give me to fight with.

All of a sudden I was mad clean through. That son of a bitch had really been laying for me, doctoring that hogleg then tolling me over here to burn the place down! A guy who'd do that wouldn't be above shooting you in the back when he was done — chrissake, he'd practically promised! *If you're found in the ashes you'll get the blame anyway.*

He'd sure had me pegged for a boob, I thought bitterly. I guessed them bushwhackers, no matter their intentions, had wound up saving a Ranger's life for him.

Going down there now was some considerable more risky. A guy with a gun had at least half a chance. If I got caught with this piece of junk Curly'd loaned me I could sure wind up just as dead as poor Buck.

I thumbed the loads back into the cylinder, shoved the gun in my holster and hauled out the rifle I had left behind yester-day, more than ready to believe he'd took care of it too.

He hadn't bothered.

Feeling somewhat better, I studied Bolton's layout a long five minutes, but without uncovering anything new. I couldn't from this angle see but half the yard; I couldn't see at all the part where we'd been hagglin' when the fireworks caught us. Before I went any nearer I had a powerful craving to rectify this.

Swinging Snuffy back behind a line of screening brush, I moved him cautious-like left along a downward pitch that snaked anti-godlin more or less towards the river, thankful at least I wouldn't have to cross water if this brashness stayed with me long enough to slip closer.

I was closer already. Problem now was to get another look without exposing myself, preferably without alerting anybody.

This I presently managed to do. I remembered the way Buck had pitched from his saddle, that hind-legged screech from Curly's rearing mount; but they wasn't there now. I saw that sagging damn porch, the whole front of the house.

That yard was bare as a Paiute's bottom!

CHAPTER 19

Shouldn't of give me such a jolt — not after the way Fletch Dowling had took off, but it's hard to get used to traveling corpses. Besides it didn't make sense. At least why move the goddam horse?

Time was getting away on cartwheels. I quit gulping air, knowing I'd better get after them pronto, yet continued to stare, uneasy, filled with undefinable disquiet. I just didn't like the smell of that place. If they still was there, I could lose a lot more than chunks out of my hat.

I draped it over the snout of my rifle, waggled it round above the buckbrush and greasewood. Nobody shouted nor took a crack at it. I peered some more but them buildings stayed still as things cut out of cardboard. I finally kneed Snuffy more into the open, steel-spring ready to go off the far side at the first whisper.

Nothing changed. The quiet of that yard

was like the middle of a hurricane.

Far from convinced, I coaxed Snuffy nearer, cocked rifle held ready for the first sign of trickery. Jumpy as a sack with three cats inside it we moved into the yard. Not all the way in, just alongside one edge of it, trying to watch out in four directions at once.

No tenderfoot trapper at his first skunk skinning was any more wary than the way I injuned up on that house. Once bit, twice shy. I was willing if need be to die for Cap Mossman, but only as a reluctant and mighty final last resort.

Slipping off my horse on the barn's blind side, I took a dally round the nub of my notions and, not exposing a thing I didn't have to, made a thorough job of combing them sheds before I come up against that open kitchen door.

Behind that dark maw could be my last look at anything. I listened so hard I could hear the blood slogging through each vein and artery, and that was all I did hear through three, four minutes of eyeing that door.

I nearly choked on held breath, then in a gulping rush of nerves cried: "I know you're in there! You got about three seconds to come out with your paws up an' won't be told twice!"

More silence I got. A godawful pile of it. Then, just as I was fixing to go rampaging in, dragging footsteps crossed the boards of the floor.

I don't know what I expected, certainly not what I saw. You talk about being knocked over with a feather! I reckon my eyes about rolled off my cheekbones to see that girl from Scott's peering back at me, that Mexkin, Connie, whose old man they had hauled from the bottom of a shaft.

She looked more scairt than I'd been even.

Guess I stared like a poorfarm ninny. When I did catch up enough spit to talk with, I yelled, "What the hell *you* doin' here?" so loud, cheeks blanching, she shrank back in alarm.

She stared and swallered and, eyes big as slop buckets, swallered again. "I was trying," she said, scarce louder than a cricket, "to find some theeng to eat."

"Chrissake! Ain't you got no better damn sense than skally-hoot round with a bunch of drygulchers?"

She stared like one of us had to be stupid.

"Them guys," I growled, "that tried to clobber us . . . you been with 'em, ain't you?"

She looked more stumped than a blue-tailed fly in a gob of sorghum. "I'm not see no one," she finally said, sullen.

"When'd you get here?"

"Mebbeso five minutes."

"Where's your *caballo?*"

She glared like she figured I was ribbing her or something.

"If you don't mind," I said, "I'm in kind of a hurry. Where'd you leave it?"

"I have no *caballo.*" She looked like it was my fault.

Kind of give my wits a shake, way she told it. I remembered how she had run from that store with me standing over that sonofabitch Hank. I could see how she might of kept right on running — she'd been scairt enough, seemed like. And she did look a mite peaked, now I'd got around to notice.

"All right," I said, trying to make it sound reasonable no matter my mind was off in forty directions, "I guess you been tryin' to keep outa Hank's clutches."

Wide eyed still, she give a jerky nod.

Straining like I was to get after them bastards, begrudging every wasted moment, one notion come through that made a kind of weird sense and which I'd never of happened onto without her being there to give my thoughts a shove.

Been Lockhart mostly back of all the

views I'd took of what was going on in this country — another of them things I'd picked up from Curly. Now I seen it didn't have to be him. Could just as well of been Hank, and more likely. Hank's style stood out of that goddam shooting like a purple camel in a two foot drift.

It was the kind of deal Ponchatraine would be apt for, smarting like he'd been when he pulled out of that mix with the Judge shouting after him.

Couldn't of known, of course, we'd be coming over here, but Bolton's must of looked an ideal place to bury himself and lick at his wounds with me nearby to ease them a little. Spotting us three splashing over the river he must of figured he'd hit the jackpot sure when with one fell swoop he could take care of me and get Lockhart blamed clean to hell and gone.

Then why, God damn it, had they moved them bodies!

Or, I thought smoldering, *had* they? When the trap fell apart with me getting clean, been the natural thing for them to dig for the tules. If they'd lit out straightway, who'd clean up the shambles? In spite of it seeming so damn improbable, had Curly somehow got away, too?

Curly had no reason to do Lockhart any

favors. But if all that burnt powder hadn't dropped but the one of us, you could see how Hank might have reckoned it smart to be long gone from this place in a hurry — even to scrub the slate clean before they went off to dump poor Buck in a dry wash somewheres.

"Señor?"

I growled at her, impatient. "You go on inside an' find yourself some grub while I take a look around."

Not bothering to see if she did or she didn't, I started hunting tracks, too mixed up in my head to worry overmuch how all this queerness shaped up to her. I had troubles of my own that was a lot more important.

Casting about in ever widening circles, I finally come on to where they'd took off. The yard itself had been brushed free of sign. No tracks, no bodies, not even one solitary drop of blood. It was like we'd never been near the place. Or anyone else.

Curly, if he'd got clear, might of later come back to pick up Buck, but he'd have no reason to be piddlin' around here rubbing out sign. He'd be wanting all the evidence hung on Lockhart's door — and I hadn't found nothing to suggest he'd come back. No tracks at all heading towards the river which he'd have to cross to reach Walking M. I tramped into the kitchen still fighting my hat.

I wasn't in no mood to be trimming my words. From where I stood this kid was nothing but a nuisance. Yet without no horse I was loath to leave her, and considerable more reluctant to throw away the time it would take to move her out of harm's way. She was no kin of mine and no part of my orders but what self-respecting Ranger was going to mount up and leave a female in the lurch? I wasn't in no doubt of Cap's views on the subject.

And then, before I could say anything at all, I seen the shape of her stiffen where she stood by the table, the eyes above that half-ate chicken leg frozen black with dread.

CHAPTER 20

With a cold inner quaking I heard it too, muted but loudening, pummeling the walls with increasing sharpness. The sound of running hoofs.

You'd think I'd know better, but I stuck my head out anyway to see a ragged file of riders busting down from the hills, arrowing in on this place like a dash of Comanches.

No doubt in my mind who was paying this visit. You didn't have to count to know we was faced with that kill-crazy Hank and his brood of sacked gunnies. He had suckered me neat, making out to depart after juggling them bodies, baiting his trap with this chit of a girl.

I was minded to smack her, putting on to be scairt and hand in glove with that bastard!

No chance of escape on a horse packing double that was already wore pretty near to a frazzle — even was I minded to snake her out of this bind. Hell, I knew at first glance no fool on two legs would ever make it to the barn to get onto that claybank before Hank's crowd chopped him up into doll-rags.

Jumping back I slammed the door shut, threw the bar across it, wondering fierce-like what to do next. Didn't seem like I had any great amount of choices — I sure wasn't taking off from *here* in no hurry.

Rifle slugs rattled the walls like hail and that bug-eyed girl turned gray as wood ash. Walking M, I reminded myself, was consid-erable closer than this side of Frisco. With the wind just right, the noise of them rifles could easy go that far. Only there wasn't enough wind to pick up a paper. And even if there was, who was there but Belle to hear it? Time she gathered up a crew . . .

I jerked myself away from that kind of thinking. A Ranger never quit, Cap had said often enough. But Cap wasn't here; he couldn't hear them blue whistlers. He wasn't trapped in this heat with Hank's bunch outside trying to turn him into a colander.

"Don't just stand there!" I growled at her savagely. "Them slugs ain't like to be playin' no favorites! If you got a gun you better figure to use it."

174

She said she hadn't and got down on the floor. "Poke around," I said. "Maybe you can find one," and I went toward the front, wondering how long it would take them to rush us.

Didn't make no difference, if she was with them or wasn't. A closed mouth don't embarrass nobody. She'd catch the same dose I got if Hank had his way.

At least I still had my rifle and a beltful of shells. I stood back out of the light and took a squint at the yard.

Some of it I couldn't see none too good but I got the feeling most of them out there, given a choice, would of been someplace else. Guess they'd heard how near Hank had come to shaking hands with the devil that day I'd gone in to pick up Belle's package. There didn't none of them look what you'd call rightdown eager.

They'd thrown their horses in a pen and was scattering out afoot; 'deploying' is what they'd of called it in the cavalry. Not finding Hank in my sights I picked me out the nearest and knocked him sprawling. Rest of them took to their heels like ants piling out of a burning log.

Slugs bit into the wall like hornets. One flew past near enough to whisper cousin and

175

I let go of my pride and got down on the floor.

If I could count on some help — but how the hell could I?

Belle probably knew where we'd gone right enough, but her confidence in Curly wouldn't get whittled down enough for several hours yet to prod her into maybe showing up with two, three others. If I could hold them off till dark . . .

Leastways while there was life, a guy could keep hoping. Something might turn up, I told myself, trying hard to believe it.

The firing now had got a heap sporadic with only an occasional thump at the wall. I wasn't lulled by this into any false premises. Hank wanted me dead and was in good shape to manage it. It was time I reckoned to give them another reminder of my shooting ability. I started crawling towards the hall.

It pulled at my notice that girl wasn't making no more noise than a mouse.

Without it was from fright, I couldn't think of no reason she would want to help Hank. But if she did, being out there by herself was giving her plenty of opportunity. For all I knew she could be holding open the door right now, wigwagging him in.

The spare bedroom was on the yard side

of the hall and it seemed like, suddenly, a good place to be — anywhere looked better than this wide-open hall where I could be clobbered from two directions.

I reached up for the latch, thumbed it off and eased in, knowing I'd ought to be making the rounds but seeing likewise in a place big as this I hadn't a chipmunk's chance of standing them off if Ponchatraine could talk them into rushing all sides simultaneous. I got over under the window and edged up for a peek. Two guys, as I looked, jumped up out of cover and with sixguns fisted flung themselves straight towards me. I slid my Winchester across the sill, took careful aim and let it speak.

The southmost guy let out the banshee yell of a wolf-grabbed rabbit, buckled in mid air and went down like a busted sack. The second pistol packer, before I could so much as shift my rifle, clutched at his belly and went down ass over elbows.

My jaw must of dropped a foot and forty inches. Two birds with one bullet strained even *my* belief. Then from the kitchen came the blast of a shot, louder than them outside ones and I knew that the girl had got herself armed. Heartened by this, I leaned out of the window and drove two quick ones at Hank's stunned jaspers, both clean misses

— not that it made any great amount of difference.

Hank's plans was scrapped, the whole push going hellbent for their horses, heating their axles like the heelflies was after them.

I couldn't understand it till I jumped outside and spotted a bunch of gun-waving horsebackers fogging up the lane off the Charleston road.

Even as Hank's crew — what was left of it, was piling out of that pen, another guy pitched from his horse in convulsions. I didn't see nobody stop or turn back for him. Them still able spurred away, stretching out for the hills in a great boil of dust.

The bunch off the road pulled into the yard, some of them apparently minded to give chase till Lockhart waved them back. "What was that all about?" he growled, peering hard at me.

I took him off to one side.

"Bolton," I said, "told me two, three days ago he was sellin' this place. Curly reckoned it was you, said nobody else had the price to buy anything. This mornin' he told Buck an' me to fetch our saddle guns an' we struck out for here. Your exramrod, Ponchatraine, either had him a first class inspiration or picked this place for whatever new deviltry he's got to the stove.

"He was right here holed up an' waitin' with them six he quit town with when we pulled into the yard. Curly was allowin' we'd burn these buildings when Hank and company opened up. I saw Buck go down an' Curly's horse an' decided this wasn't no place for me."

I told him how, but not why, I had finally come back, about the absence of bodies an' finding this Connie kid here from Scott's store.

He said, "I'll take care of her," like it was his responsibility, which maybe it was though you couldn't notice no stampede around here of jaspers anxious to be shouldering theirs. "I'm astonished they'd bother to hide their handiwork. By the way," he added, "I did buy this place and that's what we're here for — to get settled in."

Sometimes he was a mite hard to keep up with.

I suppose to his bosses land was land, no matter its condition or what it had on it. Did seem kind of queer to me though with things like they was, him thinking to bed down alongside Walking M's fence.

Maybe this notion was reflected in my look at him. He put on a wry smile. "You don't seem entirely overjoyed, Adams."

"Not," I said, "if you're settlin' here

personal. I'm thinkin' of Belle Bandle. You don't shuck folks of prejudice by rubbin' their nose in it."

"It's what we don't understand that generally upsets us most. Her views of me were likely brought on by Curly. Getting to know me better might change her mind."

CHAPTER 21

Trouble, you'd think, ain't a matter of places. It's people's cross-purposes, how they're put together, the notions and wants they've let get out of hand that heats up the blood and pushes them into the awful binds they get in. Just the same, riding back, it seemed like to me I'd never come to Dowling's yet without more worries than I knew what to do with.

Bad enough to picture that gore-hungry Hank hid out behind every rock and pear clump chomping to puncture my earthly envelope without being gnawed about putting Belle next to these latest calamities.

I couldn't share Lockhart's hope having him for a neighbor was going to mitigate anything. Him moving onto that road ranch was like to push Belle into doing something furious regardless of cost, the law or anything well-wishers might bring up to dissuade her. She'd not reckon for a minute he hadn't come over there to put the finishing touches on his plans for Walking M.

Sweat come out on my hands just thinking about it and Snuffy kept walling his big eyes around at me. He could tell, I guess, I wasn't feeling too chipper. Now and again he'd snatch a mouthful of weeds, ears laid back to see if I'd notice, and the nearer we got the slower he moved.

Sun bent shadows was long on the ground when we turned through the gate.

Belle came tearing across the yard. *"Where's Curly?"*

She sure set a heap of store by that guy.

Eyes wide and dark she cried, "What happened?"

"We run into some trouble," I growled, and told her. About the trap we'd rode into and me lighting out of there.

First off she didn't say nothing at all, just staring, cheeks the color of chalk. "All right," she scowled, "let's have the rest of it. Lockhart, of course — you go to town to report it?"

I shook my head. "And it wasn't Lockhart. I got more'n my share of looks at 'em later. It was Hank Ponchatraine and that crew of hardcases Lockhart fired." I told her curling lip about going back, finding that Mex kid, Connie; about Hank and his gunnies coming out of the hills, about us trading shots with them, Lockhart's arrival and the drygulchers' fight.

No question what she thought of it. Her mind was made up before I'd finished telling about the shots that dropped Buck spitting blood from his saddle. All she had room in her heart for was Lockhart.

"When are you going to wake up?" she said bitterly. "Any kid in three-cornered pants could see he was back of that whole put-up fracas —"

"You think he would coldblooded shoot his own outfit?"

"Why not?" she jeered. "They're *all* on his payroll! Ain't you got *any* sense? That hog's not playin' for peanuts — one way or another he figures to gobble up this range!"

Pumped full of Curly's notions I could see, all right, how it looked to her. But that didn't make it so. I shook my head at her.

"Grow up or get off this ranch!" she cried, beside herself, and we glared at each other through a couple long minutes.

"Two wrongs don't make a right," I said. "No matter what else he's done or ain't done, I was there in town, not ten foot away, when Lockhart told Ponchatraine he was fired, an' them other six with him. If he was the devil you paint him why would he take in that Mex kid, Connie?"

I might's well saved my breath.

"You'll see," she said, "when Curly gets back — nobody's pullin' the wool over *his* eyes."

"Curly's dead," I told her. "He ain't comin' back."

She went off towards the house without yea or nay.

I grabbed up my reins, put Snuffy into the day pen. All the time I was rubbing him down I kept turning it over, scowling and grumbling like a sore-footed squaw. She was bound and determined to equate Lockhart with the devil and though I didn't figure anyone could be black as that I still wasn't able to get my mind off it. Come right down to it she could be nearer right than I wanted to think about.

I fetched Snuffy, soon as he was done with his rolling, a hatful of oats. I forked down hay for him, cramming two armfuls of it into the feedrack before I tramped over to get myself washed.

It was easy to make Ponchatraine the bad wolf in this. He stuck out a mile as the most likely prospect, a natural born bastard. Yet I supposed if you wanted to split hairs, you could find a few things that didn't quite gee, like that longhaired galoot I had chased the other night. He *had* been in that Charleston honkytonk, and so had Lockhart. And Lockhart *had* taken over that road ranch.

All that glitters ain't gold by a long shot. I sure didn't cotton to being played for no sucker. Yet I told myself, scowling, if Lockhart was crooked I was a Chinaman's uncle.

From what little I had seen of him, the syndicate's resident manager stacked up to be a pretty square gent. He was in a tough spot with a thankless job that was bound to make him enemies. He gave the impression of doing the best he knew how. He had a lot of hard choices and it hadn't been the easiest thing for him to get up and flatfooted fire Hank Ponchatraine, yet despite what Belle thought, he had done it.

She could be right just the same, I supposed. He could of fired him for the record and still be paying him under the counter — it wouldn't be the first time a thing like that was pulled. How much of my belief in him was sprung from thinking of Sara Jeanne I wasn't prepared to tackle right then but I knew this was something that would have to be weighed. I was reminded of his bigness taking in that kid, Connie — but what better way could he have found to keep her mouth shut?

I heard the crew riding in and thought to

myself I'd better keep an open mind. Things could get a whole lot worse before they started getting better. That was another of Cap's sayings that seemed to hold a world of truth. I could of wished I had about half his experience, or somebody I could of talked to about this.

I rinsed out the bucket and put it back on the bench, listening to Coosie sliding pans across the stove. It's hard to be suspicious of a man who's saved your bacon.

Belle, over at the house, put her head out the door yelling for me like I was some kind of slave or something. Which I wasn't too keen about, but with no help for it I took myself over there.

"Come in — come in!" she growled when I rapped — and "Set down!" she said when I hauled off my hat. In a gruff sort of way she seemed strangely unlike herself; nervous, you'd think, the way her glance flew around. But she wasn't the kind to beat around any bushes. "There's a schoolhouse dance over in town tonight. We're goin'. Tell the crew — What's the matter?"

"That business at Bolton's."

"What about it?"

"Christ! You just lost a hand, not to mention a foreman! How's it goin' to look when the word gets around? You goin' to a dance practically over their dead bodies —"

Belle snorted. "Sometimes I wonder about you," she said, and looked at me hard. Then she snorted again. "Curly'll be there, don't you worry about that — he's an oak post, Adams. No gang of bushwackin' sidewinders. . . . Even if they did, we'll find it out quicker in town than in a whole month of Sundays spent stumblin' around through this buckbrush an' cactus. Goddam it, don't argue! I planned to go an' I'm goin' — what the hell do you think I bought that dress for?"

She set her head to one side, hard eyes full of challenge. "Get yourself slicked up. You're squirin' me personal."

CHAPTER 22

It was like a mule had slammed a hoof in my brisket.

Guess I gaped like a ninny, caught up in a whirl of fragmented thoughts all pinwheeling round an' anguished remembrance nobody but a plumb fool or Pearly Adams ever for ten seconds could of forgot in the first place.

"No," I gulped, trying to grab onto something, "you better find someone else. I — I just can't do it!"

She peered, too flabbergasted even to haul shut her jaw. But I could see the mad working up through her astonishment, blackly churning behind the glitter of that stare.

"Can't or won't?"

"Don't make no difference." It was a mouse's squeaky voice. I told her, sweating, "You'll have to find someone else."

You could see how rotten her old man had spoiled her. It wasn't only how she looked in them too-tight pants and bulging shirt. It come out of the very way she stood, white cheeked, cocksure, the nose on her flaring like a stallion bronc's.

I could feel the sweat trickling down my back. And I could feel Cap's badge squeezed against my leg. It give me the courage to growl back at her doggedly. "I already got this thing laid out."

With a smoldery look she said, mouth pinched: "So you've promised to take someone else to this hoedown!"

"What good's a man's word if he don't stick to it?"

"Who is she?"

"That's my affair."

Her eyes turned nasty. She said, full of venom, "When a man works for me he does what I say."

I could be some stubborn myself on occasion. It wasn't an easy choice forced on me, but: "If that's a threat," I told her, "you can tote up my time."

She went back a step, eyes wide, mouth open. "You'd quit," she cried, "just to take some hussy —"

"A man's got his pride — even a fool kid. Which is what, inside, you think about me." I give her back look for look. "I'm not a damn *peon* whatever you think!"

189

The air in that room got scarce and thin. I thought, by God, she would tromp all over me, her eyes was that wild. But she went over to the desk like a wet-footed cat, grabbed up a pen and scratched off a check. Breathing hard she spun round, holding it out to me. "There — take it and go."

Was that a sob in her voice? Was them tears that made her blinking eyes look so sparkly?

"Go — go!" she cried. "An' don't you *never* come back!"

It was nine or after time I got into town and, guilty mean, stopped off at the Chink's to buy my tapeworm a few minutes' peace. I'd had some pretty crummy jobs before Cap latched onto me, but this was the first I'd ever run out on and the kind of lost look of her holding that check out still rode me hard.

No question I'd done the right thing. But that didn't rid my mind of dark fancies or make easier to contemplate what fit she'd throw when she bumped into me squiring Lockhart's niece.

I left Snuffy at the gate. It was Lockhart himself that opened the door to me. "Well!" he grinned. "Come out of the cold and toast your shins by the fire. She'll be down in a minute — we'd about give you up."

I followed him into the light of the parlor, felt his glance sharpen. "You look like a man who's had to put away a dear one."

"Nothin' like that. I've quit Belle Bandle."

"Well, you had to come to it." The silence piled up while he studied me, nodding. "You ain't burned your last bridge, son."

"Kind of feels like the sky fell."

"I ain't gone back on what I told you. You can step right into Hank Ponchatraine's boots." His grin came back. "I'd say this calls for a celebration." He filled two glasses from a bottle on the sideboard, held one out. We heard her feet on the stairs. "To mutual profit," he said, lifting his.

I guess I needed it.

Sara Jeanne, flushing prettily under my inspection, pecked Lockhart's cheek and fetched her eyes around shyly. "No need to wait up," she told her uncle. "With Mr. Adams, I'll be safe as Gibraltar."

We let ourselves out. She asked, "Did you ever see the stars so bright?"

Suddenly inspired, I poked a thumb at Venus. "Shall I get that one for you?" Her soft tinkle of laughter was reward enough.

With that drink warm inside me and a pretty girl's approval I'd of forgot my head if it hadn't been hitched to me.

One thing I'd forgot was to fetch round a rig but she said it didn't matter. School-house wasn't over a quarter mile away. "I like to walk," she confided, slipping her arm through mine, kind of hugging it. The stars was brighter, no doubt about it.

With all the hung-out lanterns, fiddle squeal and laughter, a guy would had to be been both deaf and blind to miss that frolic. Rigs and saddlers was left all over with a lot of loud voices coming from off to one side where some merchant had set up a couple of kegs.

I took Sara Jeanne through the stags round the veranda, thinking as I did this was the only school I'd ever heard tell of that could boast a waste of wood for the benefit of shade. The bug-eyed envy aroused by our passage put a spring in my step, and I expect the knowledge — though not yet shared — of being Lockhart's ramrod might of had something to do with it. This wasn't a job like to make many friends but it could influence people and probably open some doors nothing else would budge.

I did once or twice kind of wonder who he'd left at that road ranch and what had been done about that Mex kid, Connie, but mostly I was just floating on air.

It was a real jamboree. I suspect the whole

town and half the county in one shape or another had turned out for the occasion. Everywhere you looked folks was packed ten deep, talking, laughing, whooping up a storm. There was so many on the floor you couldn't find your own set if you didn't look sharp. We danced three squares, two waltzes and a polka before the heat and exertion caught up with us. I left Sara then to get us some punch.

Took me a while to get over to the table and the jam around it would have tried the patience of a reservation Indian. Fuming and fretting while sweating out my turn, something — when I'd finally got within two hands of the ladle — hauled my stare about like the feeling of eyes boring into your back.

He was already moving, trying to lose himself in the crowd round the door, when my eyes picked out that mop of long hair falling over the collar of a faded brush jacket. Clean forgetting the punch I went hotfooting after him.

This was the joker who'd tried to nail me at Bolton's and I didn't mean to let him get away if I could help it. I got to the door shoving guys off my elbows. Ignoring scowls and curses I barged through onto that lantern-lit veranda.

For a couple of seconds I thought I'd lost him sure. But apparently he didn't even know I had seen him because there he was in no special hurry tramping like he was looking for something between the rows of hitched rigs. It was darker out there and darker still where he was heading.

I went down them steps like the wrath of God.

CHAPTER 23

A guy in a hurry can get pretty worked up and, like I found out, a whole lot quicker be cold as a dead fish. It wasn't till I'd got among them rigs myself that my hand, reaching hipward, fetched me staring to a stop.

I'd clean forgot being naked as a belly dancer's middle, having checked my iron at the door when we went in. I wasn't in much doubt backed into a corner Bolton's buddy would shoot, but I didn't twist my head. There was no use going back for that piece of junk I had got from Curly.

Tugged two ways I went cautiously forward, catfooting into the deeper dark, more wary now but twice as determined. I'd a lot to make up for as Cap would have told you and Lockhart, too, bulking large in my thoughts. Too often this guy had made me look silly. I had lost him again but he was out there someplace; I'd of damn well known if he'd got onto a horse.

Edgy, unsure, head canted I listened, hearing no hoofs, no boot scuff or anything else that seemed to hold much significance till it come over me, gradual, there had ought anyways to be a few crickets scraping. It was almost as if the whole night listened with me.

A bristling broke out on the damp of my neck but I wasn't about to be turned back now. Lowering each foot with breath held, I crept on through a gloom that seemed thicker than pea soup, feeling my way like a goddam snail, getting mighty little good from that skyful of stars we had thought was so bright outside Lockhart's door.

There was rigs all around — springwagons and buggies, an occasional buckboard or fringe-topped surrey. More than one hitched horse softly blew through his nose, turned nervous by my presence. After several more stops and God knew how many paces there came from someplace ahead the low pitched mumble of arguing voices.

I couldn't make out if this was Longhair or not. Only time I'd heard him speak was too long ago — that time he'd said at Bolton's place if I wanted a job I'd better hit up Fletch Dowling.

I worked in closer, extra careful and filled with prickles, trying to make some sense out of all that jawing, but they'd turned quieter now, maybe reached an understanding or some make-do shift of their differences. I still didn't know if that heavier voice was coming from the guy I'd chased to Charleston but the other, surprising me, turned out to sound more like a woman's; and I was fixing to get the hell away, not wanting no trouble with hid-out sparkers, when something about the way she spoke took hold of my thinking to stop me short.

I couldn't make it make sense. I told myself it didn't, that never in this world . . . But there was one way to know and jaws clamped I took it.

Peeling a match from the band of my hat, forgetting caution, I stepped boldly toward the black lump of that buggy, clearing my throat to let them get themselves straightened, convinced even then I had to be wrong.

A muttered oath came out of the dark as I dragged that match down the leg of my Levi's. Came a scramble of motion as it burst into flame.

All I saw was his back disappearing as he went plunging off, that thick mop of hair falling back across his collar and Belle Bandle's wide eyes, black as coal, staring back at me.

Stiff and unnatural she might seem as she hunched the cloak more tightly about her, but there was no sign of fluster in the cool way she said, "This is not what you think, but you were right about one thing. They did kill Curly — he even saw where they buried him, but the body isn't there now. That's what he came to tell me, and to learn what help I'd give him."

"Why should you want to help him?" I peered at her, astonished. "That's the gunnie," I said, "that's been hanging out at Bolton's. He's tried twice to kill me, once anyway that I know about —"

"He needs help," she said. "He's been holed up over there waiting for us to get him out of the country."

I felt the match on my fingers and, muttering, dropped it. She said mighty earnest, "He's no gun fighter, Adams. If he ever tried to kill you it's because he was stampeded into it by fright."

"You seem," I growled, "to know a powerful lot about him never to of mentioned him that I could hear before. Was it on his account Curly wanted to send Bolton's place up in smoke?"

I couldn't tell if she gasped, but that's what it sounded like. I could feel her staring.

She squirmed around a little, pulled a fresh breath into her. "You must be mistaken. Curly wouldn't do that. . . ."

Seemed more like she was trying to persuade herself than me. "Curly'd have no reason —"

"Who *is* this guy?" I broke in, impatient. "Why would he figure *you'd* be wantin' to help him?" Inspired, I said to the huddled shape of her: "He some old flame or somethin'?"

She did gasp then. "He's a goddam fool that just never grew up — been into one scrape right after another. His name," she said bitterly, "is Bandle — Bennie Bandle."

My jaw, I guess, dropped a foot and forty inches.

"Well, Hell's draggin' gate hinge! Why'n't you say he was your brother?"

"He's not," she cried. "Not actually, I mean. He doesn't have any legal claim on us at all; it's just that — listen," she said, and this is what she told me:

Her father, it seemed, had always wanted a boy to carry on his name and take over the reins of Straddlebug, but all her mother had ever given him was Belle. She'd tried to

199

take a boy's place but that wasn't what he'd wanted. And then one day he'd latched onto this Bennie kid, a wagon train stray from a bunch of run-out squatters. The boy was ten when old man Bandle had taken him in, thinking the kid was young enough to mold into what he wanted.

He'd been given every advantage Straddle-bug and Bandle's bankroll could hand him except actual adoption — the old man had never taken out papers, never gone through the courts. He'd used the Bandle name and everything else that was Bandle's and, if he'd stayed to home, tended his knitting, he'd have had his half of the ranch under Bandle's will.

But he wouldn't face up to things, always taking off when he could least be spared. "He'd take up with anyone," Belle said disgusted. "But he'd always come back, and all he brought was trouble. The best thing he did was to make himself out to be something he wasn't. He ran up bills, he got in trouble with girls. He stole cattle and horses, but he'd always come home, knowing Dad would bail him out and settle up for him." Then he'd killed two men and that was as far as the old man would go.

"How come he's still loose?"

"It didn't happen around here. I guess the

law never caught up with him."

It was a pretty good blanket for covering him up with but I could sense gaps and it didn't seem like enough for him to be hounding her. There was nothing soft or sentimental that I had noticed about Belle Bandle, so why would he think. . . .

I wished I could make out her face in them shadows. "It just ain't good enough. It don't quite go down. If your old man chucked him off the place why would he figure you would care what happened to him? There's got to be more than what you've told."

"Why should I tell you *anything?*" she bridled.

And that was part of it. Why, indeed?

If Bandle had kicked him off the place and right after got himself killed by a horse, as she'd told me once, getting took off like that seemed considerable to swallow the way it looked to me. Which was all the more reason to make him counting on her look fishy.

She was powerful still.

She let go of a sigh that must of come from her bootstraps. "Curly killed Dowling. Bennie claims to have seen him packing off the body."

CHAPTER 24

Now, I thought, we were getting to bedrock!

It wouldn't strain one part of me to believe anything that could be told about that feller; nothing would be too wicked. I remembered well the first time he'd set on me and what he'd been up to the last time — him and that worked-over pistol! *This* was something you could get your teeth into.

The glowering bastard had damn good reason for wanting that place burned — I had told him myself about Bennie being over there. Two birds with one match, that was what he'd been up to!

So many things were answered now. I nodded in the dark, forgetting she couldn't see me. It was this longhaired Bennie buck who'd pointed me at Dowling, asking why I didn't hit *him* up for a job. It could of been him, too, who'd put it in Hank's mind to lay for me at Bolton's.

My head was fair awhirl with thoughts set

off by Belle's revelations. I'm surprised I could see the woods for the trees but one thing stood out plain as a bonfire; whatever that Bennie had been after from Belle he still had — through Curly — enough hold on her he wasn't like to go off without trying another turn.

The next move seemed urgent and, to me, pretty clear.

Whether as Mossman's rep or stand-in for Lockhart, it behooved me to get back to Bolton's *muy pronto.* Someplace around there Bennie would be waiting to sink the hooks in her again. He wasn't an old soldier to just fade away. Them Bandles had been too soft a touch.

If I could get my hands on and keep ahold of him . . .

Belle became impatient. "Don't be feelin' so damn self-righteous. You ain't been appointed to sit in judgment. Nobody *set out* to kill Dowlin', for chrissake!"

"The courts take a pretty dim view —"

"It don't," she said, "have to get to no court. The guy's disappeared. That's all there is to it."

I peered at her, scowling. "But you moved the Straddlebug crew into Dowlin's, Straddlebug cows —"

"To keep Lockhart from takin' over. The

place *belongs* to me, I got a right to protect myself!"

"If nobody set out to kill him how'd it happen?"

"Dowlin's fence had got breached. Curly was over there movin' some cows when Dowlin' come onto him with hell in his caw. It wasn't the first time he'd found fence down. Rustlers been hittin' him harder than most — probably lost his head. Never called out or nothing, just grabbed iron and started triggerin'. Curly waggled his arms tryin' to make himself known, but two near misses was all he could wait for. He flipped up his Winchester thinking to scare the damn fool off. Dowlin' rode right into it."

I could feel her eyes on me. "That's the truth, Adams."

It could have been that way. But I said, "How do you know?"

"How do I know my name's Belle Bandle?"

"You took his word for it?"

"Right first rattle."

"Naturally he'd put the best face he could on it."

"When Curly says a thing's so you can bank on it —"

"They why'd he fiddle round hidin' the body?"

"Because he seen how it would look, this rustlin' an' all. He ain't no parlor cat. He'd been in trouble before with them Charleston counter-jumpers; if he packed Dowlin' in he'd wind up stretching rope. Only law we got is in Lockhart's pocket. He wouldn't lie to me — Straddlebug's his whole life."

Remembering the times I'd seen him come from the house I had myself a few reservations, but this didn't seem no time to air them. I said, touching my hat to her, "Reckon I'll shove along. I've got —"

"Wait a minute, Adams." I could see her bending towards me. "You ain't goin' to make an issue of this, are you? Curly had a bad enough name without that."

When I didn't jump into speech straight-away she said, reaching out, "What difference is it going to make now who killed Dowlin'? Hangin' it on Curly ain't going to bring him back."

We eyed each other through the squeal of fiddles, the tromping boots and the guitar plunkin'. I didn't say what was in my head but was riled enough to tell her bluntly: "I wasn't figurin' to shout from no rooftops, but I can't guarantee that kid'll keep his mouth shut."

"But if he's kept on the run —"

"Maybe you're forgettin' I don't work for

you no more."

"I was coming to that. With Curly gone I'm goin' to need a new cow boss. . . ."

She let it hang like a trade, like a goddam plum she expected me to reach for, and I cried, fed up: "I've got all the job I can handle right now ramroddin' Two-Pole Pumpkin for Lockhart," and turned on my heel while her mouth still hung open.

It done me good to leave her like that, to let her know some people rated me a cut above her two-bit notions. Entertaining Curly in the middle of the night!

I picked up my hat and that damn wrecked pistol, bypassed the punch, and told Sara Jeanne who wasn't looking too pleased that something had come up and I would have to take her home. She didn't throw no kind of fit, just smiled with her teeth and told me she had promised this set to Bert Klingerman who said to me, beaming, that I should run right along, he'd be happy to see she got home safe.

I returned his look without much favor, remembering his reputed bachelor status and the horse spread he run out west of Belle's place, that he was one of them jaspers she had to her meetings. He had a full face of teeth under slicked-back hair that was orangey red like a woodpecker's comb and long-lashed eyes that kept sliding around like a pair of peeled grapes.

He was a heap too hearty to suit my book and the smirk he put on like he figured himself to be God's gift to woman did almighty little to improve my outlook. I was almost minded to forget my hunch and let the damn road ranch look after itself.

I might of done it, too, only just about then while I was backing and filling trying to find the right words, Sara Jeanne like butter wouldn't melt in her mouth told this Klingerman jigger: "Be thankful, Bert, you've got a place of your own and don't have to kowtow to the needs of an employer."

That reminder of my duty, though doubly unwelcome coming from her, clamped the hat on my head and sent me doorward. Jerking tight the cinch without regard to Snuffy's feelings, I stepped into the saddle, swearing under my breath, and pointed his nose in the direction of the river.

I could of done with a gun in my belt that would shoot but where to get hold of one this time of night was something beyond the scope of my experience. I could be plumb wrong expecting trouble at Bolton's, but, remembering Belle's talk and Hank loose in the hills still gnawed by his setbacks, it looked the logical place with that dance going on for someone to let all kinds of hell loose.

As a new broom for Lockhart I felt impelled to make some kind of showing — but it wasn't just that. Cap had sent me here to clap the brakes on trouble. While I wouldn't of figured openly to help Belle for spite, I could see well enough what chance of peace there'd be for anyone with hydrophoby Bennie tearing loose through these hills. And Belle, in her present frame of mind. . . .

I felt like a guy on a lit keg of powder. Anything could happen and something was pretty near bound to.

I rode Snuffy hard with a head full of things I couldn't shake or shove aside. I had enough to keep me squirming without being prodded by badgering visions of Sara in the arms of that toothy Bert Klingerman. Even Lockhart, who seemed to have the patience of Job, wasn't like to hold still for very much more of this — or even be allowed to if Belle had her way.

CHAPTER 25

Certain facts would emerge from any situation Cap had said more than once, if a man would just back off and look at it calmly.

God knows, I tried. But facts in this jamboree appeared scarce as hens' teeth.

It was a fact Hank Ponchatraine had been forcing unwanted attentions on Connie. But what other facts was there besides the obvious one that Fletch Dowling, operating Walking M, had disappeared? For all I knew he could have *owned* the place — I had only Belle's word he'd been running it on lease.

Until Ponchatraine's outfit had snuffed Curly's light — if in fact they really had — he had loomed to my thinking the most likely to keep things stirred. Hank Ponchatraine, while mighty near certain to have been exceeding his instructions as applied to Lockhart's policy, didn't have enough wheels hidden under his hat to be the prime mover in what was going on here. He was just an overbearing gun-handy tough, in love with the picture he had of himself, quick to resent anything that disturbed it. This, anyhow, was the way I saw him, a strictly common type.

But now, touching Curly, I wasn't so sure. A lot being blamed on Hank and the syndicate could just as well have been undercover stunts pulled, or at least thought up, by Belle's dark-visaged ramrod. He had not been able to abide any part of Two-Pole Pumpkin, had seemed particularly rabid about the syndicate's choice of manager.

And there was Lockhart himself.

Had I let myself be taken in by Dallas' proximity, his blood relationship to Sara? Was he actually all he seemed? Or was there in fact, as Belle would have you think, some hidden ruthlessness snapping and snarling with wolfish ferocity behind that smooth presence?

Admittedly, he'd gone out of his way to have Hank's case against me squashed. But he had also, admittedly, wanted me on his side in this business, and someway or other that didn't appear to make sense.

You might argue that Hank had worn out his welcome, that a change of faces at the reins had seemed desirable, a buffer between Lockhart's job and these cowmen he'd come here to put out of business. But why me, an unknown, a feller too young to have had any real amount of practical experience — was *that* why he wanted me put in Hank's boots?

Out here on the range the star-spangled sky seemed to shed more light than back at that schoolhouse. Before we was two hours on the road a peculiar shine low down against the horizon, like the afterglow of sunset, began to exercise what part of me wasn't already fussed with darker things. Without really thinking too much about it, this lighter patch in the night's starry sea seemed to pulsate like the leap of flames and — if I had any sense of geography at all — looked a lot like coming from where I was bound for.

Soon enough it took over most of my attention.

I didn't snatch up no fencepost to whale more speed out of Snuffy nor rake bloody tracks across his flanks with my spurs. But it wasn't because I wasn't anxious to get there or out of any kindness I might have for dumb animals. Like most people's reasons, shorn of excuses, it was based on self-interest. I didn't want to ride into no life or death bind on a horse that didn't have an ounce of run left.

It looked like the worst of my fears was realized. I couldn't doubt that brightness was coming from Bolton's. While I was still some forty minutes from getting there, the last of that flare frazzled out of the sky.

I was following the river like I had that first time, keeping clear of the hills on the shortest course I knew. And all the while it was plain I wouldn't get there in time to make one ounce of difference.

It was a hard piece of knowledge for a Ranger to chew on — a guy Cap had sent here to stomp the lid on trouble. I took what comfort I could from knowing if I'd run Snuffy's hoofs off it still wouldn't have changed anything that had happened. I still couldn't have got there quick enough to have turned the outcome.

At least they hadn't set the whole range afire.

I guessed what wind there was had been blowing away from Walking M — not that this would have made any nevermind to a bullypuss jigger like Hank Ponchatraine. I did wonder, though, what precautions Lockhart had taken to protect this foothold he had bought — or presumably bought — in Straddlebug's stomping ground. Had he left the full crew he'd used to run Hank off?

Since I didn't know his mind on the subject, I couldn't guess how deep he had figured to be involved. Them ramshackle buildings and whatever sliver of land went with them, must look a first-rate base for any kind of dido aimed at putting the squeeze on Walking M. Surely he'd of left . . . unless, of course, he was the kind Belle claimed, in which case maybe he had bought the place for bait, knowing how it would burn her gizzard, hoping perhaps her bull-headed ramrod would tie on something he could take into court.

I didn't know what to think. He didn't seem that sort to me. I didn't want to believe he was, but again it was Sara's face I was looking at mostly. The pull of Sara Jeanne could be powerful distracting.

I hadn't heard no shots and on account of the wind — what little was blowing — I didn't smell no smoke till I got pretty near within two miles of the place. It come from Bolton's all right. I pulled down to a walk, keeping both eyes peeled, ears standing out like the handles on a jug.

Didn't seem too likely, but there was a possibility whoever had hit that spread was still around and I sure didn't hanker to make bait for coyotes.

There wasn't much left, time I got a look

at it. A couple stone chimneys, smoldering joists, the half of one wall not built of wood like the rest of it. Smelt some ranker than you'd get from a wolf den. There was a half roasted horse showing about ten foot from where the house porch had been, but no amount of hard looks cast round and about was able to find any sign of life.

I sat listening to the crackle and fitful snap of them smoldering timbers for a considerable spell before, some reluctant, I swung down to poke around. There was a pair of charred shapes in the part that had been the barroom. That was all the corpses I come across though I spent the best part of at least thirty minutes scouring the vicinity hoping to turn up something or someone that might give me a line on the parties responsible.

Looked like Lockhart hadn't left but two men. If they'd knocked down anything besides that one horse, the surviving raiders must've toted it off. Hank, if it *was* Hank, had made a clean sweep, even to cutting the hull off that broomtail.

There was no way now that I could check up on Ponchatraine. He'd be holed up somewhere out in the hills and I would play hell searching out tracks short of daybreak.

I had no intention of sticking round that long.

Them bodies was evidence, not to be tampered with, but one thing anyhow I reckoned I could do. There was nothing to stop me going to Walking M. Under the guise of fetching news I could have me a look for bandaged limbs or, anyway, count noses.

Rejoining Snuffy I climbed into the saddle. He looked no more anxious to sit up with them stiffs than I was.

I took hold of the reins then turned, still listening. Some scrape of sound had come out of the dark. Hoof thuds walked off the river trail and I dragged my rifle clear of leather, throwing it up at full cock, heart thumping.

The moon in that moment crossed the top of the mountain and there was this other guy, stiff as I was, not a rope's length away, crouched in his stirrups hands clamped to a rifle, peering, mouth open. I could almost think it was me in a mirror.

CHAPTER 26

Except, of course, the guy peering back wasn't *me.*

I don't know which of us was most startled. Breaking loose of that stunned inspection we both tore into words simultaneous: "Supposed you'd gone to bed," I growled. Lockhart said, "I thought you was with Sara Jeanne at the schoolhouse!" Both of us shut our mouths, both glared.

Dryly Lockhart suddenly chuckled, "Hit I guess by the same hunch I was."

My cheeks felt stiff enough to crack nuts on. "I left Sara Jeanne with Bert Klingerman. You must've took off before that shindig was over."

Lockhart sighed. "Plain stupid of me — things like they are — to have gone back to town leaving only three punchers to hold up my end of this. Got to thinking about it right after you left. I was heading for the stable when Sid Havens showed with word they'd been jumped."

"Why'd you come off alone? Reckon just the sight of you was worth a thousand guns?"

Lockhart chewed at his lip long enough to get his wind back. "I figured to be too late for help to make any difference. Havens killed a horse gettin' there — bad shape himself. I left the doc workin' on him."

"What'd he tell you?"

Lockhart looked at me, bridling. "You talk pretty large for the size of your navel." Then, shaking his head, he growled, "Let that go — guess I'm kind of on edge myself." He sighed again. "He got out of here fast — he'd been over to the barn looking after a sick cow. Too many, he reckoned, to be stood off. Tried to give them others what chance he could by making a run for it. Guess he did pull a few of them after him a ways."

Seemed plausible enough, I thought, to hear him tell it. "Havens say who it was?"

"Couldn't even guess. All had their heads covered over with gunnysacks."

"How many did he think?"

Lockhart shrugged. "Conditions like that, everything dark and the yard full of movement, three, four guys whoopin' and hollerin' could sound like an army."

"So it could of been Hank's bunch."

I could see Lockhart peering. He grumbled dryly. "Be light before long. We'll have ourselves a look at what's round here."

Neither him nor me had yet put up our rifles. I said stiff-necked: "You don't reckon *I* was mixed up in this thing, do you?"

"I'll not say," he smiled, "it didn't cross my mind when I got that first look at you. With so much talk flying round about range roughers, you'd have had to been somethin' less than a halfwit not to have done some wondering about *me*." He did laugh then and put up his saddle gun. "One of the hardest facts a man has to live with is the amount of suspicions stirred up in this world. We have to take some things on trust, don't we, son?"

I tried to see him without prejudice, but her face stood out plainer with that toothy Bert grinning over her shoulder. I forced myself to remember it had been Lockhart mostly behind all the views I'd took of what was being pulled off in this country. They'd hardly put a fool in charge of syndicate expansion. He had to be some shrewder than he'd shown himself to me.

"By the way," I said, putting up my own rifle, "how'd you like to trade pistols?"

Surprise was evident in the way his tipped

head watched me. "Mine," I said, "ain't plumb reliable . . . not if you hired me with gunplay in mind."

Gruffly mumbling, he kneed his horse over, holding out his iron. It wasn't the sort of thing a man would do if he was the kind these loudmouths painted. Feeling some guilty I handed him the gun I'd got off Curly.

It was kind of a dirty trick to be pulled by a Ranger on a man of his standing and I was minded, account of this, to warn him about it; but before I could nudge myself into doing so a rumor of hoof sound, muzzy and muffled, come up off the river, sharply turning the both of us.

There was nothing for a handful of moments to see in the light that overhung the shore in drifting tatters of fog. But the sound loudened, coming steadily nearer and obviously caused by more than one pony. With a look chucked at me, Lockhart snaked out his rifle, a move I was edgily quick to follow, wondering what devilment would be onto us now.

We didn't have much of a wait before, in the strengthening light with them stingers of mist standing over the river, a solid blotch of horsebackers bulged into sight to break apart sudden-like and come swinging towards us.

Not till they saw the glint of our Winchesters did their leader fling up a hand, stopping them in a skidding half circle. Their boss was Belle, in pants again, and she looked pretty shaken, I thought, peering across at us.

"Right neighborly of you to come to our assistance," Lockhart said, breaking out a smile. "Got kind of chilly so we had us a fire."

"Thank God it wasn't our place!" Her eyes wheeled to me, ignoring him. "What are you doin' here, Adams?"

All the old arrogance was back in her voice. No mention of what *they* were doing on this trail. I said, "You better be takin' some pills for that memory. I told you in town I was workin' for Lockhart. Where's the rest of your crew?"

She looked around, seeming surprised not to find them all with her. Not bothering to answer she demanded to be told how the fire had got started. "Syndicate been gettin' a dose of its own medicine?"

I said, "Why don't you listen for a change when people talk to you?"

"Want me t' bust him one, Miz Belle?"

That was one of her bunch. I scarcely give

him a glance. "Mr. Lockhart has just told you. We was tryin' to keep warm."

"All that believe that can stand on their heads. Where's the crew you left on this place?"

"How'd you know we left a crew here?"

No sign of her being taken aback. Teeth gleamed behind the curl of her lip. "You'd of had to been ready for the boobyhouse not to!" She picked up her reins. To Lockhart she said, "I hope they rub your damn nose in it!" Without more ado she kicked her mount into motion, the rest of her outfit wheeling in behind, but not before I'd looked again, sharp this time, at the whippoorwill who'd asked to hang his knuckles on my jaw. Though he wasn't one of them I'd worked with I had a pretty strong feeling we had met before. And as they rode from the yard I placed him.

It was the pot-gutted hairpin who'd been pardnering Bennie the first time I'd seen him in Bolton's bar. The jigger who'd been hustling him out of the place when he asked why I didn't hire out to Fletch Dowling.

"You ever run into the longhaired galoot who's been hauntin' these parts under the name of Bennie Bandle?" I asked Lockhart after they'd gone.

"Don't believe I have," he said with his

eyes screwed up like he was searching his memory. "Heard of him, of course. Kinda bad egg, wasn't he?"

"Could depend which side of the fence a guy looks from. He's still around, by the way. He might of killed Dowlin' or be tied in to whatever happened to him." I went on to tell of the times me and that longhaired galoot had crossed trails. "He's the one I was after when I banged into you. He was siftin' around through town last night, was at that schoolhouse, out by the wagons, havin' a confab with Belle."

Lockhart rubbed at his jaw, considering. "Maybe we better look around here a little."

CHAPTER 27

We cut for sign, done a heap of looking, without being no amount forwarder than before. We found where them gunnysackers had tore through the yard, even discovered where they'd come swooping out of the hills. We didn't find no evidence they had been cut up any. Only things we proved by all that labor was there hadn't been but four of them.

It still could of been part of Ponchatraine's bunch. There wasn't nothing to show these wasn't syndicate riders carrying out Lockhart's orders. Only thing really against either one of these conclusions so far as I could see was the fact that when Belle come riding through a while ago, four hands had been missing from her outfit, including Coosie.

You'll be wondering why I'd told Lockhart it might of been that wagon train stray who'd put the finger on Dowling when the girl had definitely told me it was Curly had killed Fletch and packed off his body. Well, I wasn't swallowing the kitchen sink. I figured she said a heap of things besides her prayers, if any.

I had got to the point where I distrusted everyone, inclined to take their mouthings with considerable more than a sprinkle of salt.

Belle made no bones what she thought about Lockhart; right from the start she and Curly between them had made him look a second cousin to Lucifer. She sure wouldn't want him camping at her fenceline.

It had been Curly's intention to burn his place almost quick as I'd told him Bolton was selling. And Curly and her, when it come to big Dallas, thought about as much alike as made no difference. She was cram-jammed plumb full of hate and defiance.

It was hard, I'll admit, to think of her coldbloodedly consigning to that fiery grave a pair of syndicate punchers she didn't know from Adam. It was Belle, after all, who had kept that goddam Curly from stringing me up when they'd found me in Fletch's house.

But she didn't *have* to have ordered them killed — she could simply have let it be known she'd be glad if that place would catch fire some night. I'd been considerable amazed they hadn't burnt it long since. Place like that wasn't no good to anyone without it tied in some way with this rustling. I would bet anything you cared to name Dowling's cows had been lifted by way of this hidey hole.

Well, it was burned now. No doubt about that. And she looked good as any to have been the one behind it. And, touching back to Bennie again, what proof did we have he wasn't the one who had done for poor Fletch? Only Belle's tell of it! It wouldn't be the first time I had caught her in a whopper!

Lockhart spoke with a weary sigh. "Might as well be shaking a hoof, I guess. Coroner's got to be told about this and we'll have to get hold of the sheriff's man. I don't mind too much the material loss. From what I've heard this has been a rats' nest ever since they stopped runnin' stages through here. But I sure hate the way them two boys had to go."

When we got back to our horses, Snuffy snorted his impatience.

"Who," I asked, "do you figure was back of this?"

"That'll be up to the sheriff." He didn't look round. "I rather doubt we'll ever get it pinned down. We can take steps, though, to make sure . . . Tell you what —" he climbed into his saddle. "Our closest base from here is Bar T. You pick up a crew and come back here with rations; throw back every critter that's not packing our brand. Thursday you can look for a herd to play round with. I'll be throwing twenty-five hundred head in here."

I bit down on a swear word and looked at him hard. "I don't know how much range you picked up with this place but from what I can see, it won't support two hundred cows."

Lockhart grinned. "You catch on real fast."

Snuffy pawed at the ground but I paid him no mind. I guess I hadn't really seen Lockhart before. The gall of his announcement went through me like a dose of salts.

"You can't mean that!" I got out finally. "Why it would —"

"They want trouble: by grab we'll give 'em a bellyful. And all perfectly legal."

Now I was seeing the other side of him, the reason, no doubt, he'd been picked for this job. He had more steel than a iron horse and what he said was the truth. There was no laws against it. He could put all the cows he wanted on this place.

If they didn't stay on that was no fault of his. Cows have to eat. They eat whatever they can find — boundaries don't mean nothing at all. Fences can be pushed over.

I knew damn well he wasn't saying this for laughs. But I had to try anyway. "What you're proposin'," I said squeakily, "will start guns bangin' —"

"Won't be the first guns you've ever listened at."

"But, Jesus Christ, Dallas! It could've been that Bennie that burned this place —"

"He never done it singlehanded."

"So maybe he had help. You want a shootin' war on your hands?"

"Them fellas went into this with both eyes open. We ain't playin' drop-the-handkerchief, Adams! We got hit, we hit back. And we don't fool around with it — hit 'em in the pocketbook you make a real impression. Burnin' this place was a overt act."

He smiled like a Santa Claus without his beard. "I've seen this comin'. That Belle Bandle has been tryin' for weeks to talk the rest of them into pilin' the grief on me. Man's got a right to protect himself. Time to stop trouble —"

"Is right damn now!" I looked him straight

in the eye. "I won't go along with this. There's been enough trouble now."

He said, half humorous, "You pullin' out on me, boy?"

"That ain't all I'm doin'." I fished Cap's badge from my boot, pinned it glinting on the front of my vest. "If there's any more shootin' gets loose around here, somebody's goin' to catch a free ride to Yuma!"

His eyes was some narrower but I didn't find anything that looked like fright in them. "Not namin' no names? Well, that makes sense, I guess. Pinnin' the tail on the donkey could be a mite of a chore for a galoot in strange country with no help to fall back on. Ain't nothing in your by-laws says Rangers can't have accidents, is there?"

Neither one of us took his look from the other. "Well, here's wishin' you luck," Lockhart said to me finally. "Man all by himself is a heap apt to need it."

I didn't know if it was smart showing my hand to him like that, but nothing else I could think of held out any hope for changing his mind. Maybe this wouldn't, either, but I was getting fed up with all this pussy-footing round. Coming out in the open, if it didn't get me killed, might jog loose a few of the answers buried back of the things that had been happening here.

When Lockhart left he was cutting across the range in the direction of Bar T. After stewing around for maybe ten minutes I got on Snuffy and pointed him for town.

It was time I laid down the law to these bastards.

I still didn't know if it was Hank Ponchatraine that was behind most of the rough stuff; he was sure behind some of it. With this new picture I had of Lockhart's character he could of, when you come down to it, been the mainspring himself. That was the popular view of it, all right. But it could also be Straddlebug, with that girl feeling like she did and Curly for a ramrod. Or it could be that peckerneck Bennie! Lousing things up for whatever he could get out of it, he would sure be my choice for the cow stealing round here!

I had plenty to think about. Hadn't had much time to think about hunger but on this trip into town my gut give me fits. And I still wasn't sure of one thing about Dowling. Pin that where it belonged and a man might make progress. Belle had dumped it on Curly, calling it a accident, but that didn't make it so. Curly, dead, could inherit a heap of things. I couldn't see, though, why she'd lie to help Bennie.

One thing seemed likely. Making my real job public sure as hell ought to smoke something out of the bushes! Whatever spider was lurking in these weeds wouldn't be wanting no Ranger sniffing into this. I was ready by now to take a calculated risk. Let them know I was Cap's man and wait for someone to try and get rid of me.

It was the only thing I could think to do.

About an hour short of noon — I'd took my time riding in — I put Snuffy into the main drag of Charleston and, star on my vest standing out like a lighthouse in that bright blaze of sun, got out of the saddle in front of the doors I'd gone through to smack Lockhart.

Leaving him hitched I went through them again.

The apron took in my badge. His mouth flopped open. I said, "You got any paper? Piece of butcher paper'll do — 'bout a yard of it'll suit me — and hurry it up, huh?"

Tramping off through the curtain he come back with a wrinkled bit about two foot square. He and me was the only ones in there.

"I'll be needin' some tacks to put this up with."

Taking a cartridge out of my shell belt, smoothing the paper out on the bar top and chewing my tongue, I drew me up a proclamation; not so fancy perhaps as the one Phil Kearny hung out in Santa Fe, but reasonably certain to command passing interest.

I took the tacks he fetched and, borrowing his hogleg, stepped outside. "Hang onto that door while I hammer this up."

Banging them tacks into place with that gun butt made enough commotion to round up an audience. I handed his gun to him over the tops of the louvered doors. When I stepped back to admire my handiwork there was enough people around to make fairly certain my remarks wouldn't go unnoticed.

WARNING

THE UNDERSIGNED GUARANTEES THE PEACE OF THIS TOWN AND ENVIRONS. ANY FURTHER ATTEMPTS TO CHANGE THE STATUS QUO WILL BE DEALT WITH SUMMARILY INCLUDING CONSIDERABLE DISPATCH.

Pearly Adams
Arizona Ranger

I had reckoned this would get results but sure wasn't expecting when I turned around to find myself ringed by the grinning faces of Hank Ponchatraine and the hard-cased

six Lockhart had dumped from the syndicate payroll.

CHAPTER 28

Expect I aged several years in them seconds.

That Hank had notions, and vicious ones, was all too apparent in the size of his grin. It was plain he was thoroughly enjoying himself and the pall his presence had thrown over the surroundings. He was the kind to glory in the breathless quiet and stiff-held stances of the sprinkling of townsmen looking on with dropped jaws.

"Got you dead to rights this time." He gave a belly-shaking guffaw. "You damn sure ain't a-goin' to wiggle outa this one!"

I put the best face I could on it. "You're wanted," I told him, "in connection with the death of the Mexkin they fished out of that mine shaft. Might's well surrender peaceable. No sense you gettin' the rest of 'em shot up, which they damn sure will if they get in my way."

Ponchatraine hooted. "Hear! Hear!" he

sniggered. "You figurin' t' do this all by yourself?"

"I'm not here to play games with you, Ponchatraine. Unbuckle that shell belt and get ahead of it quick or you're on your way to an early grave."

"By Gawd," someone whispered, "that fool really means it!"

Even Hank, seemed like, had begun to believe. He had everything his way, all the edge he could ask for — six tough guns to back him up, and both my hands full length at my sides. But my eyes, hard on him, saw sweat put its slick across the jut of his cheekbones as the worry crept through the fading laugh wrinkles.

I guessed he was remembering the other time, the jag of cloth I'd took out of his sleeve.

But he was too far along to back down from this now; he'd be rode out of town if he didn't go through. It showed in the desperate twist of his stare. Then he was reaching in a wild blur of motion and I glimpsed the lifting snout of his gun.

I squeezed off one shot and his face fell apart, incredibly surprised, as the slug threw him back on buckling knees whose hinges snapped to drop him gagging in the dust.

His six standbys stood frozen in shock,

splayed fists rigid, not quite touching their guns.

I moistened stiff lips. "Anyone else thinks I'm bluffin'?" Somebody drew a shuddering breath. One of them six begun to shake like with ague. I said, "Without you boys crave more of the same, latch onto your hats with both hands an' hang tight to 'em."

Bogy Red come up on the run, panting and puffing like a windbroke horse. "What — what — what's goin' on?" he gulped, and must of spotted my star the way he put on the brakes. I kept my stare where it would do the most good. He said kind of gruff, "You arrestin' them jaspers?"

"Not really," I grunted. "Just seemed a good idea to get 'em out of harm's way if you'd be willin' to put 'em up for a bit. They look pretty tuckered. Maybe you ought to liberate them from some of that excess weight that's hung onto 'em."

The old boy kind of grinned, then chuckled. Ignoring their protests he collected their hardware. "You wanta give me a hand?"

"Gladly," I said, slipping a fresh shell into Lockhart's pistol.

After we got them comfortably settled, all snugly latched to the pit stake with leg irons, I asked Bogy Red if he'd any idea where I could locate Connie.

He looked at me queer. "Y' mean that little Mex gal what used to work in Scott's store?" When I nodded, he said, "Understand Mister Lockhart, on behalf of the syndicate, took up a collection to kind of tide her over till she got straightened out. She bought a ticket to Juarez. Left on yesterday mornin's downcountry stage."

I found a place to eat and put away enough steak and hash browns topped off with pie and java to pack a wedge between my backbone and belly. I wasn't at all sure I liked the rush with which the syndicate's resident manager had got that Mex kid out of his hair. I would like to have talked a bit further with her. Cap Mossman didn't relish reports that left anything to the reader's imagination. A real stickler he was for tucking in loose ends.

Well, I couldn't go after her and — in my hurry to stay on top of that business — I had put Ponchatraine where shouting at a stone wall would fetch as many answers.

With my after-grub smoke, a five cent cheroot, I got to thinking about Bennie and that pot-gutted gent I'd first seen with him in Bolton's. They might not have all the answers but I reckoned they could throw some light on the subject. Spotting that guy with Belle Bandle and crew had shook up a heap of thoughts I hadn't had previous.

One thing was sure. I'd get nothing out of Lockhart, nor could I figure to find much welcome calling at his place now I'd quit him — probably wouldn't get past the goddam door.

I took Snuffy down to the public stable and hired myself a renter. He had earned a rest and I needed a mount that had built up some go and wouldn't identify me far as you could see him. I got myself a lineback dun that stood good chance of blending with the scenery. Then I set off for Walking M, riding the river to keep me out of sight till I got onto the trail that would take me past Bolton's. Guess it was more from habit than any reason I could name.

The hard-to-lay-hold-of Bennie looked bound to have some of the things I wanted. There'd been four of them fellers, so I couldn't see how the fire could be charged to him. From what I had heard he couldn't scare up three friends, though this didn't necessarily prove he hadn't been there. The sooner I met up with him the better I figured to like it.

I found no one around when I pulled up the dun in what had been Bolton's yard. I hadn't much expected to, not imagining Lockhart could get a crew here from Bar T short of nightfall. Which wasn't as far off as I might have wished for. The two stiffs was gone from where I had seen them and the tracks of a wagon seemed to indicate how. Someone from town, like enough. Coroner probably.

I put the dun into the river. We splashed across and I lined him out toward Belle's headquarters, not looking forward to my probable reception.

It wasn't too great a distance as you may recollect. I had just come in sight of the Walking M yard with the sunbent shadows blue and long across its horse tracked dust when a slug whistled past my face yelling cousin.

I quit that hull like a ruptured duck, left grab hard clamped to the stock of my saddle gun — a futile gesture as I mighty quick learned when a racket of hoofs took some-one through trees like hell wouldn't have him.

There was a draw opening out of them squatting cedars and, back in the saddle, I went into it spurring. All I got for so much wasted energy was a look at his tracks. Then I lost them on hardpan. Two side gulches, one left, one right, and both bound for the hills, presently offered me a choice, but without tracks to guide me it was anyone's guess which route he'd taken. Growling "To hell with it!" I kept on up the draw and come onto Belle less than five minutes later.

She was on a stopped horse at one side of the trail. Her eyes mightn't of been quite as big as saucepans but you could tell by the way she'd glommed onto the rifle she stood ready to give a good account of herself. I don't know who she expected but the fact it was me wasn't bringing no overjoyed grins from her direction.

"Must be goin' someplace with a chunk of coal," she observed with her lip curled. "Sounded like the whole Apache Nation on the move — you git run off your reservation, Adams?"

I hadn't no time for her pleasantries. "Bennie go past?"

She said with her stare coming up off my vest, "You're the fastest job switcher I've known in a coon's age." She peered at me curiously. "Couldn't you an' that range hog git together on how to shove honest folks off their land?"

"Bennie!" I barked. "Did he go by here?"

"My, ain't you the stern one! I haven't seen Bennie since you broke up our pow-wow at the schoolhouse last night."

I must have showed my frustration. Her eyes looked amused. "You figurin' to offer him a job with the Rangers?"

I swung my hired horse around. Whether she was lying or not — and I wouldn't of put it past her — there was no good hoping to catch up with him now. Hell, I wasn't even sure it was Bennie I was after. It could of been that pot-gutted jigger. I described him to her.

"Kettle Belly Haines," she said. "What about him?"

"He work for you?"

"That loafer! I wouldn't give him the time of day."

"He was in the bunch you come by with at Bolton's."

"That's a crime?"

I said, scowling, "He's been hangin' round with Bennie."

"That's about his speed. Got a shack south of Klingerman's, the most useless hombre you will ever come across. Curly always figured he was on the rustle but we never could catch him at it."

Walking my renter back to her yard with her the both of us was silent. It was pretty near dark. The cookhouse lamps made a cheery shine. "There comes the boys now," she said, staring past me. "Might's well feed your face while you're here."

I guessed if I didn't do it no one else would.

CHAPTER 29

As a meal it wasn't a heap on the noisy side.

The ones who'd come in all spoke or sent stiff-faced nods in my direction but nobody broke his back being friendly or ruptured himself trying to keep the talk going.

Half of them likely was nursing hangovers but there was more here than that. More than any awkwardness the badge might have wrought. You could feel the distrust hanging over the table and a darker, colder something that put me in mind of the way things had felt at Bolton's that first time when Bennie and that pot-gut had walked in. There was the feel of grit between your teeth.

Even Coosie had a kind of nervous, unsettled look.

And the whole crew hadn't showed, I noticed. Apparently Belle still had some of them on guard, patroling the fence, keeping an eye out for trouble.

Mostly this bunch kept their stares on their plates, wolfing their food like they'd got pressing business and figured to waste no time getting at it.

First three to finish got up and cleared out without even reaching for their prayer books and Durham. This left — besides myself and Coosie puttering at the stove — only four others holding down the benches.

Four seemed to have a special magic in this vicinity, turning my thoughts once more back to Bolton's. No matter how you cut it, that place appeared joined as naturally to this as eggs with hogs' meat. Same guys was missing from cook's table tonight that hadn't showed with Belle when her outfit come out of that river mist this morning. Pot-gut hadn't come to sample the grub, either. Of course she'd said he wasn't working for her.

More for something to say than for any clearer reason I asked through the clack of chomping and eating tools, "Whatever happened to the rest of this crowd? Brill, Ollie Schultz, Red Neck an' Heffron?" Looking across shoulders to address myself at Coosie, I continued, "Don't recollect seein' 'em with Miz Belle at Bolton's."

Coosie swallowed a couple of times, grabbed up a skillet, cheeks looking bunchy as a board of pounded dough.

It was one of the four sitting round me that answered. "Expect they're gettin' their licks in."

"Thought maybe they'd got a bellyful an' quit."

"We ain't got no quitters on this spread, Adams." Glowering he pushed out his jaw to say mean like: "There's places I've heard tell of where stickin' yer nose in when it ain't ast fer kin git a guy clobbered in mighty short order!"

I peered at him, chuckling. "Ever try to kill a Ranger?"

In the gasp that went up Coosie, with a dying calf look, cried like the squawk of a rusted gate hinge. *Why don't you git on your horse an' git outa here?*

I was astonished to discover he was sweating real leaf lard.

Some uncomfortable notions got loose in my noggin but, like a damn dimwit, I had to hoorah them. "You don't figure Bennie'll like it if he finds me bedded down here?"

Until right then it hadn't entered my mind that ringtail lizard might be sure enough expected, but one look at their faces didn't leave half a doubt. Coosie's eyes rolled up as though he looked for the roof to drop. These were run-of-the-mill hands. It showed in their expressions.

I got onto my feet, standing over them, scowling. I damn well hadn't figured on nothing like this.

"You rannies would let him get away with it? Puttin' the squeeze on Belle like he's doin'?" My eyes must of stuck out near as much as theirs did. I rounded on the mouthy one. "After all that big talk? She told me about that business last night but it never occurred to me nobody round here would lift a hand to help her!"

In the squirmy silence a sound of fading hoofbeats rolling back from the stable area told its story of the three who'd gone out. "Pullin' their freight," I sneered. "What kinda guys are you?"

Coosie, over by the stove, wailed. "You don't *understand*?"

I understood Curly'd been the driver on this spread, that without his blistering tongue and black scowls this crew had gone to hell in a handcart. I remembered him well and all his follies but at least, by God, he had held them together, made them a force to be reckoned with.

I stared in disgust at Coosie's stricken face. "You chipmunks sure as hell take the cake!"

The mouthy one, gone red in the jowls,

jumped to his feet full of spit and fury. "Any guy with the sense Gawd gave a gopher would of quit this outfit soon as it happened — take a look at this gun before you start pitchin' names around!"

He banged his hogleg down on the table with a spleen that made the whole place rattle.

I stared at that iron suddenly colder than frogs' legs, remembering the one I'd got off Curly. A whole heap of things dropped crashing into place as I thumbed back the hammer, saw the filed-off pin.

I must of looked a prize boob. I pulled the jaw off my chest and met their looks squarely.

Hoofs came into the yard walking soft as the sound of spider's feet and I spun toward the door, digging for my blue lightning. Two arms clamped round my chest. "Don't be a goddam fool!" Coosie hissed. "You'll be dead so quick if you step outa that door you'll think the goddam sky has fell on you!"

I shook him off and the mouthy one growled, "It ain't just Bennie —" and one more picture flipped through my head, the four who'd been missing from that river-bank visit with Belle this morning. Brill, Ollie Schultz, Red Neck and Heffron — all with the stamp of the gun fighter on them.

It was strange I hadn't ever noticed it before, but it made sense now, that fire — all the rest of it. It made Ponchatraine's bumbling bravado understandable. He hadn't never been more than he was when I'd dropped him, a second rate lead-chucker swollen like a puffed-up toad by exploits most of which he'd only took credit for.

The real bad actors was right here on this spread. Them undercover four, groomed and coached by that glowering Curly.

"Douse the light," I said.

In the dark Coosie whispered, "Don't be a damn fool! The odds, man —"

"A Ranger don't count odds," I growled, taking hold of the door.

A door shut quietly across the yard and the mouthy one said, "He's gone in to chin with her."

I went over what she'd told me about him, about Fletch Dowling's death and him putting the bite on them, but I couldn't see her handing over no money.

I pulled open the door. Coosie swore. I wasn't half as anxious to go out as they figured. Like Hank, I had a rep to live up to, but another sharper face in my head was the thing I was looking at. Nobody let Cap

Mossman down. Do or die was the code of that outfit.

Coosie groaned. "At least we kin help — you'll own to that much!"

I was watching the yard, grimly searching the shadows. I knew what I proposed was crazier than popcorn. I probably wouldn't get half across the yard but — using Lockhart's iron — with luck I might take a few of them with me.

No talk floated round. Not a breath of wind disturbed the deep quiet. One thing I knew — I wasn't up against amateurs. Doctoring them cow prodders' pistols would have told any halfwit that much. These was tough cookies, already dug in and put there to get me.

Bennie was the bait. I had to cross that yard to get at him and, the way things stood, I had about as much chance as a June frost in Tucson.

There was long gobs of light coming through the house windows but this bunch wasn't passing up any bets. Two lighted lanterns had been hung from the roof of that porch making damn sure they'd have a promiment target. There was nobody in sight, but enough black patches fringed the yard to hide any number of drygulching bastards.

I could feel the itch of sweat on my palms and rubbed them against the legs of my pants, thinking back to past times, a dozen things I'd rather do.

Ears suddenly sharpened I heard whispers behind me, scuff of furtive movements and scrapings like cloth dragged across wood, intermingled with a series of thuds which told me Coosie and the rest of them was taking their picket pins off through a window.

So much for the help I'd shamed cook into offering. "Adams," I said, "you got to do this yourself," and lifting my pistol, stepped through the door.

Nothing moved in the shadows. You'd of thought — if you was fool enough — the place was as deserted as the night I first got here and walked through that empty damn house hunting Dowling.

Step by step I moved into the yard, feeling the light on me, expecting any second to get whacked by a bullet. And still nothing happened.

It was pretty disconcerting. How much edge did they want for Christ's sake.

Like a lot of new brooms I put a value on dignity, something I hadn't ever had before Mossman. I couldn't see myself bounding over the ground in the rabbity jumps of some goddam kid. I was frightened, sure, but more scairt I guess at showing scairt than of finding myself being measured for a coffin. Cap had drilled it into every one of us boys that fright was a luxury no Ranger could afford. "Run scared and you're whipped before you ever get started."

I was going to run anyway — I could feel it coming. I'd took all I could when a shout slammed across that yard from the stables and two shots burst red from a corner of the house.

All hell broke loose in a sudden burst of yelling that seemed to be coming from every place at once. Gun thunder bounced off the fronts of the buildings as I flung myself forward in a zigzagging crouch. Muzzle lights winked from the shadows and Coosie with a singletree gripped in both fists reeled out of the smithy and went flat on his face.

I nailed the guy at the house's near corner, sent Heffron spinning with a slug through the shoulder. I didn't stop to count misses — was two jumps from the posts of that porch when suddenly the whole damn world blew apart to send me ass over elbows.

I scrabbled myself up out of the dust, things still whirling, to see that pot-gutted Haines charging round the far end triggering like crazy. Blinking the blur from my stare I drove a shot, saw cloth jerk just above his beltline and squeezed again on a empty click. But he was through, folding over his hurt he hit the ground like a sack of dropped oats. I staggered onto the boards and wrenched open the door.

Belle, white cheeked, was in the front room standing over dead Bennie with a smoking revolver. Her eyes met mine like she couldn't believe it.

I saw the glint of her teeth, had to strain to hear. "I was wrong," she said, "about Lockhart. It was this skunk all the . . . Well, it's over," she shuddered.

"Not quite," I said, and her stare come back.

"Bennie?" Above the grimace her eyes searched my face. "No jury in the country — he practically *forced* his way in, kept ravin' an' rantin'. Not a cent, I told him. Damn fool wouldn't listen, kept tryin' to get his hands on me. Hell, *he walked right into it!*"

"Not just Bennie," I said, shaking my head, and caught the way her look changed. "You're the one killed Dowlin'. Like enough, like you said, Bennie saw it. That's why you had to take care of him — maybe Curly, too — all the rest of it." My gun was empty but how was she to know? "I got to take you in, Belle."

The lips curled back off the shine of her teeth. "One more dead fool won't make any difference!"

She threw up her gun and I jumped, reaching for it. She fought like a wildcat. In the midst of our struggles the thing went off and I felt her go slack, the whole lumpy weight of her sagging against me.